THE

CAPTAIN

AND THE

COUNTRY COUSIN

A Regency Romance

by Mary Kingswood

The Captain and the Country Cousin

Published by Sutors Publishing

Copyright © 2021 Mary Kingswood

ISBN: 978-1-912167-40-1 (paperback)

Cover design by: Shayne Rutherford of Darkmoon Graphics

Author's note:

this book is written using historic British terminology, so *saloon* instead of *salon*, *chaperon* instead of *chaperone* and so on. I follow Jane Austen's example and refer to a group of sisters as the Miss Wintertons.

The Captain and the Country Cousin

About this book: *the dashing soldier, the earl's niece and the secret admirer...*

Lucinda Willerton-Forbes is quite content to be the useful unmarried niece, so busy organising everyone else that she gives no thought to herself. As for marriage, she isn't much bothered because she hasn't yet met a man who won't bore her to death within a month. But during a big family celebration, someone manages to enter her locked room every night to leave anonymous love tokens on her pillow. That's not boring at all, but whoever can it be?

Captain Michael Edgerton isn't looking for a wife, and Lucinda is above his touch anyway, no matter how beautiful and desirable she is. Besides, she has other, more serious suitors, far more worthy of her. But the more he gets to know her, the more he is drawn into her life and can't bear to see her throw herself away on someone who only wants to take advantage of her. Protecting damsels in distress will get him into trouble one day.

This is a complete story with a happy ever after. A stand-alone traditional Regency romance, drawing room rather than bedroom.

About Captain Edgerton and Mr Willerton-Forbes: Captain Edgerton, formerly of the East India Company Army and later of Tattersall's, and lawyer Mr Willerton-Forbes first met in *Lord Augustus,* book 3 of the *Sons of the Marquess* series, when they were helping the Duke of Dunmorton with his late son's affairs. The two became friends, and found themselves working together on a number of murders and other crimes and mysterious events throughout the *Sisters of Woodside, Silver Linings* and *Strangers* series.

The Captain and the Country Cousin

Dates and times: For those who like to know, the main part of this story takes place after the end of the *Sons of the Marquess* series, and before the first book of the *Sisters of Woodside* series. The Prologue and Epilogue take place during the *Strangers* series, between books 2 and 3. It can be read on its own, however.

About my books: Here's a complete list of my series to date and proposed:

The Daughters of Allamont Hall (6 books + a novella)

Sons of the Marquess (5 books + a novella)

Sisters of Woodside Mysteries (5 books + a novella)

Silver Linings Mysteries (6 books + a novella)

Strangers (6 books + a novella)

The Mercer's House (6 books + 2 novellas)

Want to be the first to hear about new releases? Sign up for my mailing list at http://marykingswood.co.uk

Table of Contents

The Willerton-Forbes Family

Hi-res version available at http://marykingswood.co.uk

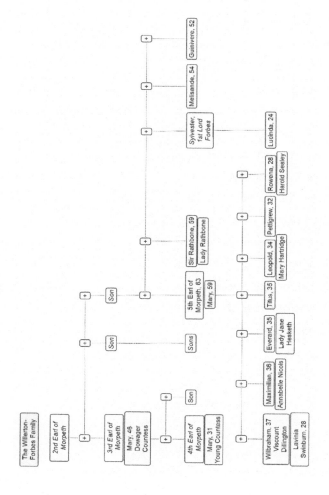

Prologue

Lucinda stared out of the window at the steady downpour of rain, and sighed. Was there anything more dismal than days of continuous rain? It was supposed to be summer, but it was hard to believe.

"You miss him," Lavinia said.

"Of course I do," Lucinda said, turning to her friend with a smile. "I am never quite happy when he is away from me."

Lavinia shook her head. "Then why do you let him go?" The sleeping baby on her lap hiccoughed, his pudgy arms waving momentarily, before he settled back into slumber. "He is always dashing about here, there and everywhere, leaving you lonely, and do not deny it, Lucy, for I can see it very well. I am very glad that you are free to come and stay with me, but I would much rather you were with Michael."

"He needs to be active," Lucinda said, coming back to the chair she had only just abandoned, and picking up her sewing. "You know what he is like, Lavinia — there is too much energy in him to be confined by domesticity, and I would disrupt his work if I were to follow him about like a puppy dog. So he goes away, he misses me abominably and then he comes home, and we have our honeymoon all over again."

Her friend laughed, looking across at her own husband, fast asleep on the chaise longue. "I can see how delightful that must be, although I confess, I prefer my husband at home with me. Mine would never stray from my side at all if I did not chase him out of the house occasionally. Look at him — only forty and already he likes an afternoon snooze, just like his mother." She smiled fondly at him, and as if he were aware of her regard, he opened his eyes, and stretched, swinging his legs to the floor.

"Shall I take the little fellow back to the nursery?" he said. "That Christening cap will never be finished if you sit and hold him all day."

"I like to hold him," she said plaintively. "He is so sweet just now, and I know perfectly well that if I take my eyes off him for a moment, he will instantly turn into a grubby little boy who would rather be climbing trees than come within a mile of his mama." She heaved a sigh. "But I suppose you are right. Take him away, Will, but do not be dawdling in the nursery. You will see the girls at the proper hour later."

"You are a cruel, unfeeling wife," he said, kissing her on the nose. "How fortunate that I love you to distraction." He swept the baby into his arms and marched triumphantly out of the room.

Lavinia had gone rather pink. "He really should stop being so sentimental. It is most unbecoming in a future earl."

"You love the way he dotes on you," Lucinda said.

The Captain and the Country Cousin

"Yes, I do rather, and I would not wish him to grow any less fond of me, but one expects a man to be more restrained after several years of marriage. Whereas Michael—" She reached for the Christening cap, and bent determinedly to her stitchery.

"Whereas Michael is *too* restrained, is that it?" Lucinda said softly. "It is quite all right, Lavinia, you may speak freely."

"Lucy, he tells everyone that he only married you for your fortune!" Lavinia burst out. "I *know* that is not true, but there are those who know you less well who are quite taken in by it, and think him a cold, unfeeling man."

"What do we care what people think?" Lucinda said, impatiently. "He is the most romantic of men. He does not speak of his feelings, not even to me, but he shows me his affection in a thousand little ways."

"Romantic? Is he?" Lavinia said. "He is such a flamboyant character that one would suppose he would court a woman openly with flowers and poetry and *passion*, Lucy, yet I had not the least idea there was anything at all between you when we all stayed at Hurtsmere Castle. He treated you no differently from anyone else — perhaps with a little more distance, if anything."

"Oh, there were flowers and poetry, and passion, too." She smiled softly, remembering. "Do you want to hear the whole story?"

"Ooh, yes!" Lavinia's eyes shone eagerly. "Wait, let me send for tea and cakes, and then we can settle down for a lovely long coze, and you can tell me all about it."

1: The Captain

SEVERAL YEARS EARLIER

AUGUST

Lucinda Willerton-Forbes took the letters to the Lesser Chamber of Hurtsmere Castle, where the three countesses sat. Lady Morpeth was snoozing, as was her wont on hot afternoons. The Dowager Countess had a book open in front of her, and was taking notes, as usual. Mary, Lady Morpeth, known as the Young Countess, was busily engaged in stitching a tiny gown for one of the babies and talking incessantly at the same time. Lucinda smiled fondly at the three of them. Three Lady Morpeths under one roof was an awkward business, especially when all of them were called Mary, but they managed well enough.

"More acceptances," Lucinda said cheerfully. "Oh, and something from Pettigrew. Wake up, Aunt Mary, do. There is a letter for you from Pettigrew."

Lady Morpeth woke at once, and stretched out her hand for her son's missive, while the others fell upon the great heap of neatly inscribed letters on the silver salver.

The Captain and the Country Cousin

"Oh, he is coming for a visit," Lady Morpeth said excitedly. "At last! And bringing a friend, too... a Captain... something. Oh dear, I hope he is not one of these dashing half-pay officers, who will distract all the girls we have invited for Titus. Lucy, can you read it? Pettigrew writes so small, sometimes."

Lucinda took the letter from her aunt, and perused her cousin's elegant script. "A Captain Edgerton, formerly of the East India Company Army," she said. "Pettigrew says he is a card player, and Uncle Quentin will be pleased to meet him. There now, that is good news, and an extra gentleman is always welcome. Pettigrew says that he knows that we will have the castle full to the brim, so the captain may share his room. The bed is more than adequate for two, and if he dislikes sharing, there is a chaise longue."

"That is all very well," Aunt Mary said, with a sigh, "and I shall be very happy to see them both, you may be sure, for gentlemen will be in short supply, but Pettigrew will have his man with him, and his coachman and groom, and two more horses to be squeezed into the stables."

"We shall manage very well," Lucinda said calmly. "The carriage may go off to Pollard End, and another valet can always be fitted in somewhere. He will have to be, for Pettigrew cannot manage without him."

"Are we making a great mistake, Lucy?" she said plaintively. "It will all be such an upheaval, and everything at sixes and sevens and the servants upset and I do so dislike Lord Morpeth to be made uncomfortable."

The Captain and the Country Cousin

"Uncle Quentin will be perfectly content so long as he has someone sensible to talk to. He will be very happy to see Pettigrew again, and hear all about the Duke of Dunmorton, the parts that Pettigrew was too discreet to consign to paper."

"We all want to hear about *that* business," the Dowager said, looking up from her pile of letters. "Marrying again at his age! And he held some kind of competition to choose a bride, and then threw them all over for frumpy Emma Frensham, and she is increasing already, did you hear? There is life in the old boy yet." She chuckled throatily, and the Young Countess laughed too.

Aunt Mary did not laugh. She still bore some vestiges of her less exalted upbringing before her husband's unexpected elevation to the peerage, and found such discussion unseemly. "We will all be happy to see Pettigrew again," she said firmly, "and his friend, too, this Captain... whatever it is."

"Edgerton, Aunt," Lucinda said. "Captain Michael Edgerton."

~~~~~

Pettigrew Willerton-Forbes was the youngest of six sons, and although all of them had taken up the law as a profession, Pettigrew had eschewed the traditional family occupation of attorney, and had gone to London to become a barrister, entering the chambers of his distinguished uncle, Sir Rathbone Willerton-Forbes. London had given him the polish that his brothers and father lacked, and the stylish man who stepped from his carriage, cane and fashionable beaver hat in hand, would not have looked out of place in Bond Street.

The Captain and the Country Cousin

His doting parents, who had not seen him for many months, fell on him with little cries of glee, and it was left to Lucinda to greet his guest. Captain Edgerton was not a tall man, being a little shorter than Lucinda, but he cut an imposing figure. His correct country attire of buckskin breeches and top boots could not disguise the powerful muscles of the habitual horseman, and his driving skills were attested by the garish blue and yellow striped waistcoat of the Four-Horse Club. One hand rested on the hilt of his sword.

"Good day to you, Captain," Lucinda said. "Welcome to Hurtsmere Castle. I am—"

"The Honourable Lucinda Willerton-Forbes," the captain said, with a wide smile before executing a flourishing bow. "Your cousin has already told me of your manifold charms, and I can see that he did not exaggerate in the least. Your servant, madam. But how is that we have not met in London? I thought I knew all the accredited beauties."

There was a warmth to the roguish gleam in his eye that made her smile. Here was a man who would always make her smile, she suspected, through sheer charm. His flirtation arose from good will and a cheerful disposition, she felt, rather than any low motive.

"I never go to town if I can help it," she said, as she rose from her curtsy. "I am a little alarmed by your sword, Captain. Are we to expect an attack? Should we raise the drawbridge and prepare the boiling oil?"

His smile widened even further, if that were possible, so that his teeth gleamed in the sunshine. "I like to be ready for any eventuality, ma'am. My sword has been my constant companion for so many years that I feel quite naked without it."

"We cannot have you feeling naked, sir," she murmured, and he laughed outright.

By this time the earl and countess had reduced their effusions over their son and turned to greet their guest, and after introducing his friend, Pettigrew turned to Lucinda.

"Lucy! How are you?" he said, kissing her cheek. "You look very well."

"I am always well, as you know. Nothing ever ails me. Your friend is an original, I think."

"Edgerton? He is, but a very good fellow, very amusing. Father will like him, for he plays an excellent hand of whist."

"So long as he does not interfere with the matchmaking for Titus. He is rather dashing, and Aunt Mary is concerned he will be a distraction."

Pettigrew laughed. "He swears he will only marry a woman of great beauty, fortune and noble rank, so unless you have such a paragon here, you are safe. No, he is only here to amuse the company. He will leaven this dull gathering a little."

"Dull gathering? A betrothal celebration, and a fortnight of matchmaking? You have no soul, Pettigrew. It will be the most immense pleasure."

"To the ladies, perhaps, and to such of the gentlemen as like to court, and the rest will no doubt occupy themselves in a variety of energetic outdoor pursuits, but the only pleasure it affords me is the sight of my family."

The Captain and the Country Cousin

"You could have seen us any time this past year, had you been able to tear yourself away from London," she said mildly.

"I have left London more than once, when duty calls," he said. "Northumberland, Yorkshire..."

"Ah, yes, such grand friends you have now, Pettigrew. Dukes and marquesses and who knows what besides."

"I would hardly be so presumptuous as to call them friends," he said modestly. "Well... perhaps one or two of the lower members of their noble families, who were particularly gracious towards a nobody like me."

"Hardly a nobody," she said tartly. "You are an Honourable, Pettigrew, and your father is an earl now, for all he wishes he were still an attorney. We are both of us Honourables now."

"I used to be so impressed that you were an Honourable," Pettigrew said. "Now I am one too. It is very hard to get used to, and mixing with the nobility on... well, not equal terms, precisely, for one can never be equal to a duke, but *accepted* by them. It is most gratifying. Ah, thank goodness, we are going inside. It is a trifle warm out here."

"It will not be warm inside," Lucinda said acidly. "It is *never* warm inside."

There was no need to show Captain Edgerton to his room, since he was to share with Pettigrew, but Lucinda chose to do it anyway. "I am sorry we cannot accommodate you as we should like, in one of the royal apartments, Captain," she said. "Unfortunately, the castle will be as full as it can hold, and we could not contrive to juggle the arrangements."

"Do not give it a moment's thought, Miss Willerton-Forbes, for I can sleep anywhere. I should be perfectly happy to bed down in the straw with the dogs in the Great Hall." He chuckled. "Not that you have them, but one feels there *ought* to be dogs and straw in the Great Hall. How delightfully medieval this place is. I feel quite at home." He pinged a suit of armour with one finger as they passed it on the stair. "Yet one wonders who the attacking hordes might be in deepest Hertfordshire. Most of our castles were build to deter the rampaging French or Welsh or Scots. I imagine the greatest threat here is a pig escaped from its pen."

"You have discovered our little secret," Lucinda said. "It is an utter sham. The second Earl knocked down the old manor house and built this monstrosity instead. No moat or drawbridge, and not a single aperture for boiling oil."

"A sad disappointment. But please tell me you have a spiral staircase or two, at the least."

"Oh yes! We certainly have *those*, and authentically draughty passageways and smoking chimneys, too. We had the snuggest little house imaginable at Pollard End, with every modern convenience put in, but here there is not even one bell pull in the house. We are obliged to station footmen everywhere. And this place is so *cold,* Captain Edgerton. Stone is never warm, even in the height of summer, and a thick shawl is a lady's most treasured garment."

Lucinda was kept busy for the rest of the day as carriages arrived in a steady stream, so it was not until everyone gathered in the Great Chamber before dinner that she saw Captain Edgerton again. He had left off his sword and his evening attire was very stylish, and rather flattering to his very manly figure. Even so, he still looked every inch the soldier, as if his horse awaited, ready for him to ride into battle. But perhaps he was one of those men who liked to look the part, but when put to the test was just as craven as any other man raised in civilised society, knowing more of the drawing room than the battlefield.

He could certainly tell a good tale, or perhaps spin a yarn would be nearer the point. He held a small group rapt with some nonsense involving tigers and a rampaging bull elephant which a lady — a lady! — took down with a single shot, and yet he made it all sound perfectly believable. When they moved into the Great Hall for dinner, Lucinda was engaged in ensuring that every guest was settled beside someone who would be a suitable companion, so she was the last lady to be seated. She found a smiling Captain Edgerton holding a chair for her.

"My dear madam, will you do me the honour of sitting beside me? I have very long arms and promise to reach for you every dish you desire."

Laughing, she sat and found that he was as good as his word, keeping her well supplied throughout the first course, even though his arms were not above average length. He was an excellent conversationalist, too, contriving to keep Aunt Melisande, on his other side, transfixed with all the latest London *on dits* regarding the Royal Family, while entertaining Lucinda with more tigerish tales.

The Captain and the Country Cousin

"I cannot make you out at all, Captain Edgerton," she said eventually. "You regale us all with the most outrageous stories, and whether they are true in every particular or partly true or not true in the least is more than I can tell, and do not much care, for they are very entertaining. However, they are all of other people. You say nothing of your own exploits. Have you no tigers or wild bull elephants in your own history?"

He smiled. "How gauche it would be in me to boast of my own adventures, Miss Willerton-Forbes, even supposing I had any worthy of boastfulness."

"I am sure all our brave soldiers in India have heroic deeds they could relate, if they so chose. How long were you in the East India Company Army?"

"Twelve years, from the age of sixteen to twenty-eight, and most of it not in the least heroic, I give you my word. Nine parts of a soldier's life is sitting about waiting for something to happen, or journeying to where it might happen, or else clearing up after it has happened, and when it *does* happen, it is not at all the sort of thing one wishes to remember when in company with a beautiful lady. Tell me instead of the riding in these parts. I have never been in Hertfordshire before and cannot wait to explore. In which direction might the best prospects be found?"

Lucinda accepted the change of subject without demur. "To begin with, you might care to ride the track around the park's perimeter. There are some splendid views to the north and west, and a long open stretch on the south side if you wish to gallop. A complete circuit is about eight miles. If you wish to go further afield, one of the grooms will show you the best ways."

"Grooms are such taciturn fellows, I find. One cannot have a conversation with a groom."

"Rowena's husband rides most days. He would be happy to—"

He gave a little shake of the head. "When gentlemen ride together, the outing becomes nothing but a means of exercise. One does not stop to admire a view or listen to birdsong or dally beside a river. One goes out, rides and returns again, often without a word spoken. Whereas when ladies are of the party, the ride becomes an excursion, and thus a pleasure in a multitude of ways. There should always be ladies in a party, so that however dull the scenery, there will always be an object of beauty to admire. Do you ride, Miss Willerton-Forbes? Might we get up a party of both sexes, and make an outing of it?"

"I should be happy to organise such a party for you, Captain, if you wish it, but I shall have no time for such pleasure myself. The final and most important guests arrive tomorrow, and the day after that we hold our celebrations. I shall be fully occupied in ensuring all goes smoothly."

"It is a thousand pities, but I suppose you cannot leave everything to the servants for such an important occasion," he murmured, but he seemed unperturbed by her refusal, and spent the rest of the meal entertaining her with anecdotes about the people he knew in India.

~~~~~

The Captain and the Country Cousin

The next day started badly and grew steadily worse. The scullery maid had let the kitchen fire go out, so there was no hot water and no oven hot enough for bread. Breakfast was late and the guests who had managed to get themselves dressed and downstairs milled about disconsolately, while those still in their rooms rang their handbells with increasing impatience and sent footmen rushing up and down stairs with enquiries. Lucinda, who had washed without fuss in cold water, found herself running about like a housemaid.

Late in the morning, the betrothal party arrived in a procession of seven carriages, and the footmen unloading luggage managed to drop a trunk. Since they were half way up the stairs at the time, the trunk bounced all the way to the bottom, flying open and scattering old Mrs Hesketh's belongings on every step. It was Lucinda who joined the embarrassed footmen in retrieving everything, and trying to stuff every last stocking and fan back into the trunk.

She found Captain Edgerton on his knees beside her. "What splendid stays," he murmured in her ear, picking up a voluminous garment large enough to house the Prince of Wales. One of the footmen sniggered.

"Hush," she whispered to the captain, snatching the stays from his grasp and pushing them hastily out of sight.

"Is this place always so delightfully chaotic?" he said with his charming smile. "I shall make it my home immediately, if so."

She smiled back, stuffed a final gown of puce brocade into the trunk, and sat back on her heels. "I hope you will not be too disappointed if I say that this is an anomaly. If the

The Captain and the Country Cousin

Willerton-Forbes family has a defining characteristic, it is dullness. As far back as our history can be traced, we have never done anything of note. One or two so far forgot themselves as to become judges, especially on the Forbes side of the family, and one has been knighted, but generally we are nonentities. And that is precisely the way we like it."

"What about your father?" he said. "If I understand the way things work, he must have been noble to make you an Honourable."

She laughed. "Yes, and much good it did him! He was a diplomat, and the King made him a baron for services to the crown, whereupon he promptly went off to France, fell into a tavern brawl and was killed. So much for his famed diplomatic skills! There, that is that disaster dealt with. Let us hope there are no more."

"You do not believe that troubles come in threes, then?" he said.

"I am not superstitious, Captain, and today I have not the time for any more catastrophes. I am looking forward to a quiet afternoon followed by a good dinner and some pleasant conversation."

Not an hour later, Aunt Guinevere had a seizure.

The rest of the day was a blur of medical men, weeping women, solemn-faced men, and servants who went off to fetch something and returned without it, or brought, unasked, something not wanted, and otherwise loitered in the passageway outside Aunt Guinevere's room, talking together in low whispers and getting in everybody's way.

The Captain and the Country Cousin

Late in the evening, long after dinner was over, Lucinda went to the Grand Chamber, where everyone was gathered, to give a final report on the patient. The card players were settling in for the night, but most of the rest were yawning, and ready for bed. As she was leaving the room, Lucinda found Captain Edgerton holding the door open for her.

"Have you eaten this evening, Miss Willerton-Forbes?" His normally teasing countenance was serious, for once.

"Oh yes, the kitchen sent up a tray for me."

"Will you not stay for a while? Let me fetch you a glass of wine while you enjoy a few minutes' rest with your family. You must be exhausted."

She could not help smiling at such kindly and unlooked-for solicitude. "You are very good, sir, but I am quite well. I am going to sit with my aunt for another half hour or so while the housekeeper takes her supper, and then I shall go to bed."

"Then I will not delay you. Good night, Miss Willerton-Forbes."

He bowed as she passed by, and she left pleasantly surprised by such consideration. She had set him down as a frivolous man, a rattle and a flirt, but it was clear that he had a more thoughtful side to him, too.

The half hour turned into an hour, and Lucinda was beginning to nod off before the housekeeper returned.

"Any change?"

"No, none. The laudanum will keep her settled for a few hours yet, but if she becomes restless, wake me at once."

The Captain and the Country Cousin

"Aye, I'll do that, madam."

Lucinda pulled her shawl more tightly about her shoulders, took up a candlestick and made her way through the darkened and somnolent castle, and down the main stairs. From the Grand Chamber, a burst of laughter suggested the hardened card players were still enjoying themselves. She crossed to the north-eastern tower, nodded to the footman who sat at the entrance and wearily climbed the stairs. Round and round and round, up three levels to the very top. Her room was inconvenient in many ways, but it was her sanctuary and oh, the view on a clear day!

Quickly she undressed, too tired to do more than drape her gown over a chair, then made for the bed.

She stopped in astonishment.

There on the pillow was a single red rose.

2: A Celebration

Lucinda was too tired to consider the rose, or who might have placed it there. She laid it on the side table, climbed into bed and blew out the candle. She was asleep within moments.

Betty woke her long after dawn, bringing her hot water and a cup of chocolate.

Lucinda sat bolt upright in bed. "Aunt Guinevere!"

"She's sleepin' real peaceful. Apothecary's with her now."

"I must go to her at once!"

"Mrs Philips sent word you wasn't needed. Mrs Carter from the village is coming up with her daughter-in-law to nurse her, and old Mrs Carter was took with just such an affliction, so they knows exactly what to do for the poor lady. Mrs Philips said you're to drink your chocolate and get dressed leisurely like a lady. Ooh, that's a pretty rose! I'll fetch a vase for it before it wilts. I wonder you had time to pick roses yesterday, what with all the happenin's goin' on."

The Captain and the Country Cousin

Rose? With a shock, Lucinda remembered. Who could have left such a romantic gesture on her pillow? A gentleman, surely, yet who would have the effrontery to walk past the footman on duty outside the only entrance to the north-eastern tower? No, probably he had bribed one of the maids to deliver his gift.

But there was no time to waste on idle speculation. Lucinda allowed herself ten minutes to drink her chocolate, standing on the tiny balcony outside her window and enjoying the cool air. Then she resolutely closed the French doors and entered her dressing room where Betty awaited her. Within the hour, Lucinda had dressed, looked in on Aunt Guinevere to satisfy herself that all was well there, and begun her day of preparation for the celebration.

It was perhaps the grandest entertainment the family had hosted at Hurtsmere Castle, being the first betrothal since the present earl's elevation to the peerage. Wilbraham, the heir, and Rowena, the only daughter, had married minor gentry long since, and Maximilian and Leopold had chosen daughters of fellow attorneys, all of it accomplished quietly and without fuss. But twins Everard and Titus had decided at the grand old age of thirty-five to do the thing in style, and had taken themselves to town for the season to choose brides. Everard had returned triumphant, having secured the hand of an earl's daughter, no less. Titus had been so absorbed in his brother's courtship that he had quite neglected his own, so he had asked his mama to invite as many unattached young ladies as could be found. He intended to spend the two weeks allotted to visitors to choose a bride of his own.

The Captain and the Country Cousin

With all the resident guests now arrived, Lucinda spared them no thought. Lord Morpeth and his multitude of sons would entertain the gentlemen, and the three countesses would look after the ladies. Lucinda's task was below stairs, to ensure that preparations for the grand dinner for eighty, followed by a ball for four hundred, were proceeding apace. She was not required to carry chairs or trays of glasses or chalk the floor of the Long Gallery herself, but several times an hour the butler or housekeeper or one of the footmen would encounter a problem, and then she was on hand to issue guidance.

In this manner, with matters of candles and ladders and vases and chairs and soup and flowers and lobster patties, the day passed in a flash. Before she knew it, the giant gong in the entrance hall was sounding to signal the dressing hour. Even then there were some last minute details to be disposed of, so she had to rush upstairs to dress, against a drift of guests already progressing towards the Grand Chamber. In her room, Betty had everything ready, the gown draped over a chair, and stockings and gloves on the bed.

"How d'you want your hair this evening, Miss Lucy? Not the pearls again!"

"I like pearls," Lucinda said mildly. "Something simple, that is my style."

"Everyone will be real dressy tonight," Betty said. "I heard Lady Wallasey's maid talkin' about diamonds and emeralds and such like. Maybe the garnets? That little headband of your poor mama's — that'd look so pretty with your hair. Add a bit of colour, like."

The Captain and the Country Cousin

Lucinda sighed. She should have thought about this sooner. "It is a big occasion, so I suppose I should make some effort, but the garnets are still in the safe, and I would not like to disturb Uncle Quentin to ask for them at such a moment. What else? That spray of artificial flowers Rowena gave me would be colourful."

"Or that rose you picked yesterday. That'd be lovely in your hair. Look." She reached for the rose, and laid it against Lucinda's head. "See? Very pretty, but not too showy. I know you don't like to draw attention to yourself, Miss Lucy."

Lucinda watched her suspiciously. "I did not pick it, Betty. It was left on my pillow. Did you have anything to do with that?"

"Me, miss? No, it's nothing to do with me."

"One of the other servants, then?"

"No, miss, no one would do that. I'd know if anyone did. Most like it was one of those Hesketh girls on the floor below. A right handful they are. Wouldn't put it past them to do something like that."

"Yes, very likely. They are teasing me, I daresay, but I want no repetition. Just to be sure, I shall lock the door when I go down tonight."

Lucinda was one of the last to arrive in the Grand Chamber, slipping in unobtrusively just as she preferred. The room was already crowded, and the noise level high enough to hurt her ears, so she crept around the side of the room, eyes lowered, until she found a quiet corner. She could not hide at dinner, however, and tonight was to be formal, so when the procession began to form, she went to find her place. Mr Graham Hesketh, brother to Everard's betrothed and her dinner companion, was awaiting her with an unctuous bow and an offered arm. He was a handsome man, and seemed all too aware of it.

The Great Hall was arranged as it would have been in medieval times, had the castle existed then, with a top table on a dais at one end and two long tables running the length of the room. With a little effort, it was possible to visualise the banners and spoils of war on the walls. She smiled, remembering Captain Edgerton insisting that there ought to be straw and dogs, so she added those to the picture, too. She could imagine the ladies in their horned hats and wimples, the men in velvet houppelandes and hoods with liripipes. There had been a book in the library at Pollard End showing some of the outlandish costumes people had worn then. How thankful she was for sensible modern clothes, the simplicity and elegance of the high-waisted gown, combining beauty and comfort. And men's clothes were just as—

Here she paused, her eye caught by Mr Hesketh's shirt points, so high and stiff that if he turned incautiously, he might put out his own eye. And was his jacket padded about the shoulders? His knee breeches and stockings were unflatteringly tight. Evening dress was very unkind to men with spindly legs. Unbidden, the image of Captain Edgerton rose in her mind, as she had seen him two evenings earlier — his very masculine form had needed no artificial padding to enhance it, his shirt points and cravat were moderate, and his legs... She was looking forward to seeing him dance, the better to admire them.

The Captain and the Country Cousin

As she took her place at the top table with Mr Hesketh beside her, she could not resist searching the crowds below the dais for the captain's manly figure. There he was! Far away from her, not as handsome as Mr Hesketh but his countenance was pleasing, with his ready smile and eyes twinkling with amusement. Although that waistcoat—! Still, every man might have one quirk, might he not, and garish waistcoats were clearly the captain's weakness.

Lucinda had previously endured one meal with Mr Hesketh at his father's house, and discovered that, son of an earl though he might be, he was no conversationalist. After he had paid her a few random compliments and induced the footman to pour wine for her, he seemed to consider his duty towards her done for the evening. He had spent the rest of the time either jesting with his brother sitting nearby, or else eating in stolid silence.

She had expected this meal to be much the same, but was surprised to find it was not so. It was as if he now noticed her for the first time, his attention fully on her. He began to ask her the sort of questions that any gentleman would have raised on first acquaintance — about herself, her family, her interests. It was rather like meeting him anew, for the boorish young man had disappeared, to be replaced by a genial fellow who showed a more than polite interest in her, as if he truly wished to get to know her better.

Lucinda wondered now about the red rose. It would have been easy for him to persuade his sisters to place the rose on her pillow, for they had the room below hers. If he had developed some sort of tendre for her, perhaps that had driven him to such a romantic gesture. He could not, perhaps, make his interest obvious in public, but might consider that an anonymous offering would make her more receptive to his advances. It was unexpected, for he had seemed a self-absorbed man, but it was flattering, if so. With such pleasant thoughts, the meal passed in a surprisingly agreeable manner.

The gentlemen were not long at their port, for the meal had taken so long that the guests for the ball would be arriving soon. Lucinda took her place in the receiving line at the top of the stairs, as a long stream of guests climbed steadily towards them, jewels glittering and feathers waving. She would sooner be anywhere but there, but her position as the only unmarried young female in the family necessitated her presence. And before long, she was greeting her most persistent suitor, Mr Walter Swinburn, who smirked proprietorially at her.

"How delightful you look this evening, Miss Willerton-Forbes," he said, bowing over her hand and holding it for far too long. "You are ready to dance, I presume? Might I secure your hand for the supper dance?"

The supper dance. She almost groaned. So she would have his company for the whole of supper, too. She sighed inwardly, but her smile never faltered. "Certainly you may, Mr Swinburn."

"And shall you be at leisure tomorrow? I should very much like to ride over from St Alban's to see you. We might stroll beside the lake, perhaps. It is so pretty at this time of year, and it would give me the greatest pleasure to... to..."

The group arriving behind him were pressing him hard, so Lucinda said hastily, "I shall look forward to it, Mr

Swinburn." He tried to bow, even as the crush swept him away from her.

When the dancing began, Lucinda was reunited with Mr Graham Hesketh, and discovered him to be a hesitant dancer. Although he seldom went wrong entirely, he was constantly a beat or two behind everyone else and the concept of conversation during the dance was utterly beyond him. Fortunately, there was enough movement of the dance to bring Lucinda rather better company for much of the time. One such turn brought her face to face with Captain Edgerton.

"Good evening, Miss Willerton-Forbes," he said, smiling warmly at her. "What an excellent setting you have here! There is nothing like a gallery for a ball, I believe. Far better than a ballroom."

Such an infectious smile! He was an accomplished dancer, not perhaps as elegant with his steps as some, but energetic.

"Do you think so? A proper ballroom has more possibilities for arranging the sets, but we could not use the Great Hall on account of the stone floor. Disastrous for the ladies' slippers."

"Ah, that is a consideration which had not occurred to me. Even so, *this* gallery is far more appealing to me than any ballroom. All these swords on the walls, Miss Willerton-Forbes! How I long to examine them closely."

The movement of the dance swept them apart before she could reply, but when they next came together, she said, "Do you have an especial interest in swords, Captain?"

The Captain and the Country Cousin

"Indeed I have, and in all the weapons men use to defend themselves. There are some fine broadswords here that I should dearly like to examine more closely."

"They are on the walls precisely so that everyone may admire them, I suppose."

"Ah yes, but I like to feel each one in my hand, the weight of it, the balance... to imagine how it was used in anger, and how well it would serve its owner in battle. There is no substitute for holding a sword. Looking at them is not at all the same."

They moved apart again, and not long after that the dance ended, but she smiled to think of the captain carefully removing each sword from its resting place, hefting it, perhaps taking a few trial slashes or thrusts with each one. He was an odd man, perhaps, but interesting, and she wished she might enjoy a whole dance with him.

She was claimed next by one of the many Hartridge boys. Even now, ten years after Leopold had married a Hartridge, she still could not tell one from another, but it scarcely mattered. They were all made from the same mould, so she knew she could safely ask him about his horses, or whether he was enjoying good sport at present, or how the new groom was working out. There was always some problem with the grooms, so there was constantly a new one being trained up. And if this particular Hartridge had no difficulty with his own groom at present, he would answer, "Oh, you must be thinking of Henry... or Charles... or Lucius," and the conversation would run on along the exact same lines.

The Captain and the Country Cousin

Lucinda wondered sometimes if she appeared as dull to them as they did to her. When they asked her what she was reading at present, or was her elderly mare still carrying her to the village and back, or had she any new dried flowers for her collection, as they always did, was it because they truly thought she enjoyed such conversations, or could they remember nothing more of her? They had once seen her pressing flowers, so she was forever labelled in their minds as the girl who presses flowers. None of them ever talked to her of swords, she thought waspishly.

The next dance was free, so she crept hastily away to the far end of the gallery where a few chairs were hidden behind a plinth. It bore an unnamed statue of a man with long, carefully curled hair and a cheerful hat with an upturned brim, and was of no artistic merit, its only virtue that it hid Lucinda from the rest of the room. Here she sat in blissful peace, enjoying the music, for all of two minutes before Lavinia found her.

Not that Lavinia's company was a penance in the slightest. She was one of the few Willerton-Forbes wives whose company Lucinda relished. Her family was very minor gentry from Surrey, and her marriage to Wilbraham, the oldest Willerton-Forbes brother, had been seen as a sensible if unexciting match. She was a refreshingly unpretentious person, and the unexpected elevation of her father-in-law to the peerage and the consequent raising of her diffident husband to the rank of viscount had changed her not one whit.

The Captain and the Country Cousin

"Here you are, dear friend," Lavinia said, plumping herself down on the next seat. "Hiding away as usual. Why are you not dancing with Walter?"

"He has engaged me for the supper dance," Lucinda said with a smile.

"Oh, excellent! Make him bring you to me at supper, then, and we shall have the most comfortable coze. Do not let him monopolise you. I hope you realise that he is winding himself up for another proposal?"

"I guessed as much," Lucinda said. "He told me he would be calling upon me tomorrow for a walk. How many times must I refuse him before he gives up, and bestows his hopes on a more receptive object?"

Lavinia laughed. "The trouble with Walter is that he cannot quite understand why you should refuse him. He is perfectly eligible, after all, with a good competence and not ill-favoured in appearance, and here you are, four and twenty already and still unwed."

"So naturally I must be at my last prayers, on the brink of donning a spinster's cap and will accept him purely as my sole means of avoiding a life as an old maid."

"It would be a very sensible match, in every way," Lavinia said with unaccustomed seriousness. "You know each other well, and have always been good friends. Love is not the only possible foundation for marriage, my dear friend. If Walter will not do, there are plenty more fish in the sea. You could be married soon enough if you would but come to London for the season."

The Captain and the Country Cousin

"I hate London!" Lucinda cried. "So much noise and bustle and *emptiness*. One bounces from one pointless engagement to another, exchanging meaningless pleasantries with people one has no desire to know better. If it were not for the shops, I should never go there at all."

"You enjoy the opera, I know you do."

"Oh yes, the opera — I enjoy that very much, and if I could but sit in a box with a few close friends, and not have to mingle in the intervals, I should be perfectly content."

Lavinia laughed. "You are a most unnatural creature, to so disdain society. But surely you wish to marry one day? You cannot be happy to be always at the beck and call of the three countesses."

"I like to be useful, and if I can relieve them of some of the difficulties of entertaining, I am glad to do it. I am not against the institution of matrimony, Lavinia. I would marry tomorrow if I could only find a man who inspires my affection. More than that — I want a man who excites me, someone with whom I could spend my whole life and not be bored. And where am I to find such a man?"

But later that night, when she returned to her bedchamber, she wondered if she had at last found such a man, a man able to enter a locked room and leave it still locked. For there on the pillow was a sheet of paper, inscribed with a charade.

'Take numbers unruly, transform them to one,

Then a place of such dampness that comfort is none.

If the diligent lady compiles these two parts,

35

The Captain and the Country Cousin

She will find what men do that imperils their hearts.'

Lucinda laughed out loud. It was past dawn and too late for riddling, so she slid the sheet under the pillow and lay down to sleep, a smile on her face.

3: A Proposal

Despite her late night, Lucinda woke early, filled with excitement. She pulled the charade from beneath her pillow, admiring the neat script with strong lines, and little flourishes and curlicues on long or tall letters. A man's hand, most definitely, but one with great character. She could make nothing of the riddle itself, for her head was abuzz with speculation — who had written this? And how on earth had he contrived to place it on her pillow, when the door had been firmly locked? Had he picked the lock? Was he so determined to present her with his charade?

Of one thing she could be certain — this was not the work of the Hesketh sisters. Slipping upstairs quietly and leaving a rose for her was one thing, but picking a lock? No, they could not do that. They would have slid the paper under the door. That is what any rational person would do, and she would have found it there on the floor. But to pick the lock spoke of a stronger determination and a more romantic instinct. Could Mr Hesketh have done so? He had not seemed particularly romantic last night. Attentive, perhaps, but nothing more than that.

The Captain and the Country Cousin

What about her faithful suitor? Yet Mr Swinburn seemed unlikely, for she could not imagine that his dullness might hide a romantic heart. It seemed unlikely that he had the imagination to break into a locked room. He had once offered her a flower — a poppy growing at the edge of a field, picked opportunely — but to sneak into her room and place one on her pillow seemed a little beyond him.

There was another possibility, though — two of the castle footmen had grown up on the Swinburn estate, and were old playfellows of his. He might well have persuaded them to dash about with roses, and to open locked doors. And — a dispiriting thought — they would have access to the housekeeper's spare keys, and there would be no lock picking needed. That was considerably less romantic, but more in line with Mr Swinburn's practical nature.

It was so puzzling, but exciting, too. The idea that she had a secret admirer set her on fire with speculation — and perhaps a touch of hope, too. Surely this would be the prelude to an open courtship? A few little tokens of affection and then, one day, she would meet him somewhere about the castle — perhaps she would pass him on the stair — and he would say, "Have you solved my charade yet?" Then she would know, and what then? Would she be surprised at an old acquaintance revealing a hidden side to his character, or would she be disappointed, perhaps? And what if it were one of her new acquaintances? But no, how could that be? No sensible man would go to such lengths unless he felt a serious attachment. It could not be someone she barely knew.

Having thus mulled over the possibilities, she turned to the riddle itself, but perhaps her head was still too full of wondering about the man behind it to concentrate, for she could make nothing of it. Eventually, she rang her bell three times to indicate to the footman on duty below that a maid was wanted on the third floor, and threw open her French doors to let in the morning air. The low sun bathed her in its warmth, and she closed her eyes and turned her face towards it. If ever she married, she would have to have a bedroom with big windows so that she could still enjoy sunshine and clear country air. She breathed deeply several times, then closed the doors again and went through to the dressing room to await Betty.

~~~~~

The betrothal celebration being now over, Lucinda's organisational abilities no longer occupied so much of her time. The castle reverted to its usual summer party entertainments — a leisurely breakfast in the Queen's Chamber, followed by brisk walks or rides or sport for the active, and ambles on the terrace for the more sedentary of the guests. Today there was to be a tour of the gardens for the young people, part of the campaign to find Titus a wife, and the earl's other sons were to take the gentlemen for some shooting.

Lucinda had a less entertaining day in prospect, for Mr Swinburn was to call upon her for his walk around the lake. Every year he made the same visit for the same reason. This was the fourth time, and she assumed it would follow the usual plan. They would stroll about for three quarters of an hour or so, perfectly amicably, then, about half way back to the castle, he would make his offer, she would refuse, and they would part again on the friendliest terms. He never showed signs of dejection, no matter how forcefully she expressed her rejection and how little room for hope she gave him. Somehow he seemed impervious to her disinclination to wed him, and since she could never bring herself to be other than civil, each time he went away convinced that another year would do the trick.

Her first call, as soon as she was dressed, was to Aunt Guinevere, whom she was astonished to see sitting up in bed looking as hale as she had ever been.

"Well, Lucy, you can put away your blacks, for I am not yet summoned to meet St Peter," she said with her throaty laugh. "I thought I was done for myself, and even had my will rewritten, but now I find it was all a hum. Still, I shan't change it back, and that's to your advantage, niece. I always meant to leave you a little something, and now 'tis done."

"That is very kind of you, Aunt, but I had far sooner have you than any bequest. No more seizures, if you please! You worried us so, and you missed all the fun last night."

"Was it fun?" her aunt said, raising disbelieving eyebrows. "Or did you sit in a corner by yourself, as you were wont to do as a girl."

"No, indeed, I stood up for almost every dance, and— Oh! When did you change your will, Aunt?"

"Yesterday morning. The sawbones bled me, and I felt a little better after that. Everard came to see me and asked if I wanted it done, just to set my mind at rest, for it was very out of date, what with all the children the boys have now, and Rowena too. I have added them all in, and as many more as happen along, and you, of course. Why do you ask?"

The Captain and the Country Cousin

"Because Graham Hesketh was excessively attentive to me last night, that is why."

Aunt Guinevere chuckled. "Was he so? You could do worse, Lucy."

"But if he is only interested in my dowry—"

"Lucinda Willerton-Forbes, look in your mirror and tell me if any man in his senses would *only* be interested in your dowry. Hesketh is a younger son and must marry an heiress, but that does not mean he is blind to your other attractions. One does not buy a house just for the roof, after all. Now run along. All this talk is exhausting. I shall take a little nap, I think."

Lucinda was left bemused by this conversation. Was she now an heiress? She already had a modest dowry and her father's house, and had never wanted a larger fortune. She could see the disadvantages all too clearly, and Graham Hesketh was the proof of it. There was a man who had taken no notice of her at all until she stood to inherit from Aunt Guinevere. No doubt Everard, as his future brother-in-law, had whispered in his ear, and he had set his sights on her fortune.

But there was one sure fact to emerge from this discussion — Mr Hesketh could not be responsible for her pillow gifts. At the time the red rose was placed, Aunt Guinevere had not yet changed her will, and therefore Lucinda was not an object to him, and it defied credibility that two different men were responsible for her two gifts. So while he might be accused of fortune-hunting, he must be acquitted of leaving offerings on her pillow.

The Captain and the Country Cousin

Then who on earth was it? She was no nearer an answer to that question.

~~~~~

She shared the breakfast table with Lord Morpeth and some of his sons, still keeping attorneys' hours, and Captain Edgerton, rising early with military efficiency. After checking below stairs that no crisis had arisen, she then waited patiently in the Lesser Chamber for Mr Swinburn to arrive. She had not quite an hour to wait, time enough to write three letters, when the summons came.

He was waiting for her in the entrance hall, his bow as easy as always. In the early years of his courtship, he had made an effort for these occasions, donning a new coat, and even pantaloons and Hessians one year, but now he looked just as he always did, a country gentleman to the core, smart but not too smart. If he stood beside Pettigrew he would look positively rustic, but she had never judged a man by his clothes. She knew and liked Walter as a man of solid worth, an honourable, decent man, but she had not the smallest desire to marry him.

They walked slowly down to the lake, talking over the previous evening's events, and discussing their mutual acquaintances — who looked well and who did not, who had danced and who not, who had drunk too much punch and who had eaten three helpings of syllabub at supper. Walter was not one to notice brewing romantic attachments, but he was interested in Everard's betrothal and Titus's hopes of a match, so they talked of that, too.

The Captain and the Country Cousin

"Lavinia pointed out some of the young ladies invited for Mr Titus to choose from," he said. "To be frank, I feel he could do better. He has seen what a splendid match Mr Everard has achieved, and if he would but make the smallest push, Mr Titus could do every bit as well."

"I am not sure he wishes to," Lucinda said, amused. "No one was more surprised than Everard when he attracted the attention of Lady Jane Hesketh, for he and Titus are only country attorneys, after all."

"They are the sons of an earl," Walter said, frowning. "Just because Lord Morpeth was an attorney before his elevation does not mean his sons should continue in the same low way. A man must always be looking to improve his station in life, both in his career, if he has one, or through his marriage. There are as many agreeable girls within the peerage as outside it, and every man owes it to his family to secure the best connection he can."

"Every man owes it to himself to consider his own comfort and wishes first," Lucinda said crisply. "He should not marry to disoblige his family, naturally, but he should choose according to his heart before all else, for without mutual affection, marriage must be a dismal business."

Walter laughed, but uneasily. "You have always had decided opinions on the subject of matrimony, have you not? I do not dispute the need for some affinity, but there must always be prudence, too. A solidly respectable match, with equality of fortune and situation, must always have brighter prospects than one based on nothing but affection."

The Captain and the Country Cousin

"I concede that emotion alone is a poor guide to decisions of such import," she said. "But so are fortune and situation, where there is no other attraction. I prefer to believe that equality of character and temperament make a better basis for felicity in marriage, where there is also affection."

"Yes, but—" He broke off abruptly, perhaps recognising the imprudence of discussing such a subject when he was about to propose marriage himself. Cautiously, he went on, "You are right, of course. Equality of character and temperament... does not that describe us perfectly? Lucinda, why have you turned your face so determinedly against me? Are we not perfectly suited? Our families, our friends would all rejoice in our marriage, our combined fortunes would make us independent, we should want for nothing."

"Except love," she said, stopping so suddenly that he had to turn to face her. "I do not love you, Walter, and I do not believe after all these years that I could grow to love you. I *like* you well enough, but for me that is not a sufficient foundation for matrimony. And before you protest, I do not think you love me, either. You first offered me your hand three years ago, and have repeated it every year since, yet not once did you ever speak of love."

"Is that what you want? For me to pour words of love into your ears? I could do that as much as any man, I daresay, but I see marriage as a solemn undertaking, not one to be sullied with frivolous words that mean nothing."

Frivolous words that mean nothing! That was honest, at least. She stared at him, and he fell silent, perhaps realising that he had crossed a boundary.

The Captain and the Country Cousin

"Then we have nothing further to say to each other on this subject," she said coldly.

"Lucinda, I beg your pardon! I spoke intemperately. Forgive me! Let me try again."

"No, indeed, there is nothing more to say. Your speech was the very opposite of intemperate, and if you cannot even speak to me with the semblance of passion at such a moment, then marriage is out of the question, you must see that. Pray assure me that you will never raise this subject with me again."

For a moment his mouth worked, as if he would argue with her but struggled to find the words. But then the fight seemed to go out of him. With a punctilious bow, he said, "Forgive me for any offence. It was unintentional. You may be sure I will not distress you with any repetition of my addresses in future. Good day, Miss Willerton-Forbes."

Their steps had led them to the far end of the lake, from where paths led either back to the house or towards the park boundary. Walter strode off in the direction of the house, so Lucinda turned resolutely in the opposite direction. She ought to return to the house herself, for the countesses would be up and about soon, and she might be needed, but she felt no inclination to follow meekly behind Walter.

A very few minutes brought her to the woodlands encircling the park, where at least she could be private and cool her anger in solitude. Insufferable man! And yet she would not have had him speak to her of love if he felt none. Better by far to be truthful. She had always supposed that he felt some attachment towards her, hidden deep inside, for he was a reticent man, but she had never suspected that his lack of open affection was due to an utter lack of all proper feeling. He cared nothing for her except as a suitable marriage partner! Her person, her manners, her modest fortune were a match for his own, and so he persisted, year after year, not because of the steady flame of love, but because she was still the most appropriate pairing for him. How depressing to be sought solely because of one's suitability. How hideous to never receive a single word of love, not even during a proposal, the one time when even a reticent man might perhaps goad himself into a modicum of passion. There was not an ounce of romance in Walter.

The thought of romance reminded her, with a frisson of delicious excitement, that she had the charade from her secret admirer in her reticule. On the perimeter ride, there were seats at regular intervals, so thither her steps led and she was soon perusing that strong hand and trying to puzzle out the words.

'Take numbers unruly, transform them to one,

Then a place of such dampness that comfort is none.

If the diligent lady compiles these two parts,

She will find what men do that imperils their hearts.'

The reference to numbers she could not comprehend at all, but surely she could think of a place of dampness? A river or sea, perhaps? But they were more than merely damp. Mud? A pool? A ford? A swamp? She sighed. She had never had the quickness of mind that could interpret such cleverness. If she could but show it around the company of an evening, one or other of them would be sure to solve it in no time, but it would be too awkward to explain how she came by it.

The thud of hooves disturbed her thoughts and alerted her to impending company. Within moments a horse cantered into view and she was hailed by Captain Edgerton, as he slid lithely from his mount's back.

"Well met, Miss Willerton-Forbes! I have taken your advice, you see, and you are quite right — this is the perfect place to ride."

"I am glad you are enjoying it, sir, but are you not joining the tour of the gardens?"

He laughed, and shook his head. "My information is that the outing is a matchmaking exercise, and since I am not searching for a wife, I should only be in the way. I shall join the shooting party later. That is a far more congenial excursion to me. But I disturb your solitude. I shall leave you to read your letter in peace."

"My letter?" She had almost forgotten the charade, still sitting in her hand. "Oh, this. No, I was just... well, never mind. I am done with it for now. I must return to the castle, for I am sure I shall be wanted by the countesses."

"Then may I accompany you? It is a good step from here, and if you tire, this fine fellow of mine would be delighted to carry you."

"How kind you are, Captain, but I would not keep you from your ride."

"I had always sooner have a pleasant companion than a solitary ride, ma'am."

The Captain and the Country Cousin

She acknowledged the compliment with a bow of the head. "Then your company would be most acceptable, sir. If we cut across the south lawn and the shrubbery, we will be at the stable yard in no time. Is this your own horse? I do not recognise him."

"Yes, my groom arrived with him yesterday. I was not sure if there would be room for him at first, but he has been squeezed in somehow."

"He is a beautiful creature. You are a connoisseur of horseflesh, I see, Captain."

He smiled, a warm smile that lit his whole face. "One necessarily learns a little of the matter in the army. I had a horse once in India..."

So began another from his inexhaustible supply of entertaining stories, and he continued in this good-humoured vein all the way back to the stables.

"Thank you for your company, Captain Edgerton," she said, as they parted at the stable yard.

"Entirely my pleasure," he said, with his typical flamboyant bow. "Perhaps tomorrow we might get up that riding party you mentioned, if the weather holds. Or do you prefer walking to riding? If that be so, then we should get up a walking party instead. You must have your share of the entertainment."

"I am not sure I can be spared for so long, but I will be happy to organise a party for you, Captain."

He was silent for a moment, and she wondered if she had offended him in some way, but then he laughed and said,

The Captain and the Country Cousin

"Ah, the indispensable cousin! But tell me what you like to do, when you are not needed by their ladyships. Do you play or sing?"

"Both, in fact. Not well, but with spirit, I am told."

"How delightful! Then perhaps we might have the felicity of enjoying a duet. I too can sing with spirit, Miss Willerton-Forbes. Not necessarily in tune, but with great gusto."

She could not help laughing. He was the most agreeable company, always good humoured. A rattle and a flirt, of course, but even his most outrageous remarks were amusing rather than offensive. It meant nothing to him, she knew that well enough. Had he not told her explicitly that he was not looking for a wife? If not for that, and if he had known her for more than three days, she might have suspected him of the pillow gifts, for she felt sure he was the sort of man who would be undeterred by a locked door. But it could not be him. Oddly, she was rather disappointed, for he was such an interesting and unusual man.

There were no duets that evening, at least none that involved Lucinda, for the Young Countess had sat with Aunt Guinevere in the afternoon, and professed herself concerned about a rattle in her breathing. Despite the protests of Aunt Guinevere herself, this necessitated the return of the full array of physicians, surgeons and apothecaries, for the countesses could never agree to accept the opinion of just one man. The end of it was that Lucinda had to spend the evening with her aunt, enjoying first a substantial dinner with her, then a game of cribbage, which her aunt won, and then watching her sleep. She never did get to the Great Chamber at all.

When she reached her bed that evening, there on the pillow was a stone of a pink swirling material, shaped by nature or artistry into the form of a heart.

4: A Puzzle

For once, Lucinda slept late, waking only when Betty brought her washing water and chocolate. When the maid had left, she slipped her hand beneath the pillow and found the smooth, solid shape of the stone heart. Taking it to the window to admire its delicate beauty, she found the colours bright in the sun, with a hint of sparkle in the swirling lines. It sat in the palm of her hand, pleasingly warm. On the back was set a tiny silver circlet for threading a ribbon. Did she dare to wear it? Not yet. Let her secret admirer wait and wonder.

A number of guests were leaving that day, having stayed only for the ball, so Lucinda was fully occupied for a while with farewell duties. Pettigrew was among those leaving.

"I had hoped you would stay longer, Cousin," Lucinda said, as she waited with him in the entrance hall for his carriage to arrive.

"So had I, but duty calls," he said.

"Might you be able to return later, if your business concludes satisfactorily?"

"Oh, I daresay there will be other business," he said airily. "There is always other business."

"You just prefer to be in town, I suspect," she said with a smile. "You are not one for country pursuits, after all. Have you been outside at all since you arrived?"

"When there are books in the library as yet unread? Heaven forfend! I confess I prefer the convenience of town, Lucy. Whereas you have to be dragged there. When did you last visit me, eh?"

She pulled a face. "So much noise and smoke and turmoil," she said. "We will miss your company, but Uncle Quentin will miss you most of all."

"But I am leaving Edgerton here, who is a worthy substitute at the whist table, even for a player of Father's calibre, and the ladies like him, too."

"He is a rattle, but a very entertaining one," she said. "Would he like a bigger room, do you think? We shall have one or two of the better rooms free now."

"I knew you would want to move him around, and so I warned him. He said to tell you that he is very happy where he is, and has no wish at all to leave his present quarters."

"Very well. Ah, there is the riding party leaving now." She tried not to sound wistful as the long train of horses came round the side of the castle from the stables. She was not fond of dancing, but an outing on horseback was far more to her taste. One never had to talk to more than one or two people at a time, and it was always possible to escape an unwanted companion by a brisk canter.

The Captain and the Country Cousin

They made such a colourful group, the ladies in their elegant habits with plumes in their hats, and the gentlemen in their fine riding coats and polished boots. Captain Edgerton waved cheerfully to her. A few grooms followed behind, to attend the horses whenever the party stopped to rest or enjoy the view or became mired in— "Oh! *Mire*," she breathed. "Of course."

"Lucy?" Pettigrew said. "Ah, here is my carriage at last."

Lucinda could hardly wait to see her cousin away, so impatient was she to check her charade again. As soon as Pettigrew's carriage had moved off, she raced back into the castle, dived into the Great Hall, empty and echoing at this hour, and pulled the paper out of her reticule.

'Take numbers unruly, transform them to one' — Yes! That must be *'add'*. *'Then a place of such dampness that comfort is none'* — that was *'mire'*. So the answer was *'admire'*. Laughter bubbled up inside her. It was true, then — she did indeed have a secret admirer.

~~~~~

Lucinda was deep in a serious discussion on the subject of bolsters with the housekeeper when a footman came to find her, to request her to attend the countesses in the Lesser Chamber. This was not an unusual event, for there was often a question the ladies could not resolve themselves, although generally it was just an excuse for her presence. She could not even say they wanted her conversation, for mostly her only rôle was to listen. The three ladies got along tolerably well, but they were in their own company so much that a different audience was often called for.

The Captain and the Country Cousin

Today there was a change, for the Dowager Countess Wallasey, Graham Hesketh's grandmother, was sitting with the countesses. Lucinda had long grown accustomed to her own countesses, gentle souls who sat about all day smiling sweetly or drifted from room to room, with many apologetic words whenever they summoned her. Lady Wallasey was of a different type altogether, who sat ramrod straight on her chair, leaning on her cane and gazing at Lucinda as if she were a prize cow. She raked Lucinda up and down with her quizzing glass, eventually dropping it with a *'Hmph'* that might have been approbation or might not.

"Come and sit here and tell me about yourself," she said, in an imperious tone that brooked no argument.

Lucinda took the chair indicated, but said, "There is little to tell, Lady Wallasey. I am a very uninteresting person."

She gave a rumble that might have been laughter. "I shall be the judge of that, young lady. Tell me of your father."

"He was a grandson of the second Earl of Morpeth," she said. "The third son of the third son. He joined a number of diplomatic missions, although I know nothing of where he went or what he accomplished, for he left no letters or journal. He was made a baron shortly before he died."

It was a bald recital, and anyone might find as much in Debrett's Peerage, but it got the conversation started and perhaps in a while Lady Wallasey would tell her what she really wanted to know.

"You have no brothers or sisters, is that correct? And your mother is also dead?"

The Captain and the Country Cousin

"That is so, ma'am. I have lived in Lord and Lady Morpeth's household since I was two years of age, first at Pollard End and lately here."

"Your father's house is yours, I understand."

"Yes, ma'am."

"It surprises me that I have never encountered you in town. Have you been presented?"

Lucinda smiled. "No, ma'am, I have never wished to participate in court activities, nor do I enjoy London society very much. I am much happier in the country."

After this, Lady Wallasey seemed to lose interest in her, turning her attention to the countesses, and Lucinda was allowed to return to the question of bolsters.

But an hour or so later, she was summoned to Lady Morpeth's dressing room.

"What may I do for you, dear ma'am?"

"You may sit quietly and listen while I talk to you, Lucy, for you are a sensible girl and deserve to know what is going on."

"Ah." Lucinda sat. "I believe I can guess. A little matchmaking, perhaps?"

Lady Morpeth chuckled. "And why not? None of us wants to see you shut away here for evermore running hither and thither for other people, and never a thought for yourself. Yet you are so set against town that it was a puzzle to see what could be done. But when Lord Morpeth and Lord Wallasey were thrashing out the settlements for Lady Jane, your name came up and it seemed like such a sensible solution. We have a niece we would see safely wed, and they have a son likewise, and what could be more convenient? Graham Hesketh is their second son, and although the elder boy is married, there is no heir as yet and they do not wish Graham to go off into the army and get himself killed. Far better that he settles down to fill his own nursery, and secure the line, do you see?"

Lucinda did see, all too clearly. "Convenient indeed, Aunt."

"Yes, is it not?" she said happily. "He has very little of his own, but you have Rudgewood House and a dowry besides, and Quentin talked to Guinevere and she was happy to put something into the pot."

Lucinda jumped to her feet. "Uncle Quentin *asked* Aunt Guinevere to leave me something in her will? So that I would marry Graham Hesketh? But that is... *despicable!*"

"Is it?" she said, startled. "Practical, I call it. Guinevere has been saying for years that she planned to do something for you. All Quentin did was to ask her to settle on an amount. Then she had her funny turn, of course, and we had to scramble rather to get something in writing. Poor Guinevere! Roused from her laudanum-induced sleep to sign a new will!"

"I wish you had not done so," Lucinda said fretfully. "Who knows what damage might have been done to her health? Why, it could have finished her off!"

"Oh, stuff! She is the toughest old bird in the world. She has had these turns before, you know, and always recovered very speedily. This one *did* seem a little more serious... but there, all is well, and Lord Wallasey is quite delighted with the plan, and now that his mother has approved it—"

"Has she?"

"Certainly. The Dowager was most taken with you. So now you know all about it, and may accept him without reluctance, for everyone approves it, you see."

"How would you manage without me, Aunt?" Lucinda said in teasing tones.

"Oh... we should contrive. The Young Countess has some cousins — poor as church mice, poor creatures! One of the girls would take your place very well."

"You have thought of everything," she said sadly, for it hurt that they were already planning to replace her.

Lucinda discovered at once the change in her status as a result of this manoeuvring. She spent the rest of the day in the Great Chamber with the female guests who had chosen not to go out riding, being gently quizzed by the Hesketh ladies. Lords Wallasey and Morpeth emerged from some male fastness, looking rather smug, and sat one either side of her, talking about nothing in particular but paying her an unaccustomed degree of attention. And when the riders returned, Graham Hesketh was one of the first to join the ladies and made straight for Lucinda's side. It was almost as if she were betrothed already.

She was glad to escape to dress for dinner, but even in her own chamber there was no relief, for Betty was full of wide-eyed speculation.

The Captain and the Country Cousin

"There's such rumours goin' round, Miss Lucy. 'Bout you and that nice Mr Hesketh. Don't suppose there's any truth in it. Is there?" she added hopefully.

"It is all wishful thinking, Betty, and not on my part. People see a young man and a young woman, both unmarried, and of similar rank and fortune. With one wedding in the air, what better than a second? But just because it would be... convenient, that does not mean it will happen."

Convenient... did she want to marry because it was convenient? Convenient for the Heskeths to have the second son so advantageously married. Convenient for the Willerton-Forbes to have the spinster niece so tidily stowed away. Convenient, convenient, convenient.

She had not seriously thought of marriage before. There had been no shortage of offers, but she had never fallen in love, and had never been sufficiently discontented to look for an escape. She was perfectly happy to be a glorified companion to Lady Morpeth, believing herself to be necessary to that lady's comfort, and now she found that Lady Morpeth could spare her very well. It was mortifying.

At dinner, she was unsurprised to find that Mr Hesketh was at her side again. He talked at first very agreeably on unexceptionable subjects, telling her all about the riding expedition, the inns they had visited, the churches and manor houses and towers they had seen, the numerous little villages they had passed through. After a while, he fell silent and her own conversational efforts met with little success. She could not tell whether he had simply run out of things to say, or had lost interest. At least there was nothing of the lover about him at all, which was a relief, for she hardly knew what she felt. If he were to propose at that moment, she would be unable to give him a coherent answer. She rather wished he would go away for a while, and leave her to ponder this new situation and decide rationally what she ought to do.

There was one interesting point to consider, in that Mr Hesketh had known before he arrived that Aunt Guinevere intended to leave Lucinda a bequest. His courtship was not only approved, but was being facilitated by both families. It would have been easy for him, therefore, to gain access to her room at any time — through his sisters, or the servants, even obtaining a key to her room. If so, he was a puzzle, for clearly a highly romantic heart beat inside that rather plodding public character. His manners were good, but she could not remember an occasion when he had made her laugh.

His secret nature was very different, as she found when she went to her room that night. There on the pillow was a little family of biscuit shapes, rabbits, she thought, frolicking in a bouncing line across the pristine whiteness of the pillow. She laughed out loud, and bit into one to taste it. Gingerbread! And she knew where it had come from, too — the bakery in one of the little villages the riding party had visited that day. He must have gone inside to buy these little treats for her.

But why so secretive? Why not give them to her openly, to proclaim his courtship? It was a puzzle.

~~~~~

The days settled into an awkward routine. Before breakfast, her time was her own, if there were no domestic crisis needing her attention, but at breakfast she would find the solemn face of Mr Hesketh, who would then claim her to help him find a book in the library, or to show him her collection of pressed flowers, or to walk in the grounds. Each time she found herself alone with him, she half expected a proposal and could not decide whether she most hoped for or dreaded that event, for she was still no nearer to deciding her answer.

By the time the other ladies were up, there was plenty to occupy her, and Mr Hesketh went out riding or shooting. Once there was an outing in the carriages, to which even Lucinda was invited, but mostly she stayed dutifully at home with the three countesses and some of the visiting ladies who were too old or too indolent to go out. Then Lucinda would sit silently with her tapestry, pondering her dilemma.

The evenings belonged to Mr Hesketh again, and he clung to her rather tenaciously, although he had little to say to her now, often sitting beside her for half hours at a time in silence. Her refuge was the pianoforte, and if no one else wished to play, she would volunteer to perform. She finally had her duet with Captain Edgerton, and discovered that, despite his self-deprecating remarks, his voice was no worse than usual for someone with more enthusiasm than skill. They sang some spirited songs together.

Every day ended with a rush to her room to look for another little gift on her pillow, and she was never disappointed. There was something different every night — a bunch of wild flowers tied with ribbon, or a tiny lavender cushion put in her stocking drawer, a bag of sweet hazelnuts or a single juicy plum.

The Captain and the Country Cousin

Yet still Mr Hesketh did not speak, and still she could not settle on an answer. Every time she found a gift on her pillow, she smiled and decided that she would marry him. Yet every time she saw him in the flesh, his store of conversation exhausted after only a few days, she was determined that she would not. It was so difficult.

One evening, she even wore her heart-shaped stone in the hope of provoking a response in him, some flicker of the admiration he professed so readily in his offerings. But he appeared not to notice. No one noticed, in fact. Not a single person commented on her unusual ornament, yet someone had gone to the trouble of giving it to her secretly. And if not Mr Hesketh, then who could it possibly be?

~~~~~

One morning, Lucinda woke even earlier than usual, and impulsively decided she would ride before breakfast. How long was it since she had been out on Grey Lady? How long since she had been out at all? It was a beautiful clear morning, with just a touch of crispness to hint at the autumn to come. Summer was not yet over, however, and she could not wait to be riding the perimeter track, the first fallen leaves crunching under the pony's hooves.

The air was so fresh that she gulped great lungfuls of it, exhilarated just to be alive on such a morning. But her buoyant spirits could not be sustained for long. What on earth was she to do? Should she marry this man for whom she felt nothing? It would please both families, and it was a sensible match for her. And yet... what was there to look forward to in a lifetime of silent meals?

The Captain and the Country Cousin

Hoofbeats behind her heralded the arrival of Captain Edgerton.

"Miss Willerton-Forbes, what a delightful surprise! I seldom meet another rider on my rambles. It would please me greatly to continue on with you, but if you prefer solitude, you must say so at once. I would not for the world intrude."

His words were commonplace, but his countenance was so cheerful and his smile so warm that she could not suppress a smile of her own. "Your company would be most welcome, Captain," she said at once. "You always lift my spirits."

"I am delighted indeed to be of such service to you, yet sorry that your spirits were in need of lifting. I hope it is only a small matter which occupies your thoughts — whether to buy new dancing shoes, or whether last night's syllabub was too sweet, or whether you should put on the blue morning gown or the green after your ride."

She laughed, and said, "I confess I have given not a moment's consideration to any of those subjects."

"Then let me relieve you of the need. You should certainly buy new dancing shoes, for a lady can never have too many. The syllabub was just right, and you should wear the green dress."

"I probably should not ask, but why?"

"Because it shows off your figure to best advantage," he said, with a grin. "You were right, you should not have asked."

That made her laugh again, even as she shook her head at his effrontery. "Captain Edgerton, you are an outrageous flirt."

The Captain and the Country Cousin

"No, indeed, I would not dare, or Mr Hesketh would flay me alive."

That wiped the smile from her face at once.

He was instantly contrite. "I beg your pardon, it was singularly inept of me to mention that subject."

"It is not of the least consequence," she said. "His intentions are not exactly a secret, after all. Everyone knows of it, even my maid. The two families have been conniving to bring it about, and so it will happen, I daresay. It is such a sensible match, after all. I cannot think of a single reason why I should not marry him."

"Do you want a reason?"

His words hung in the air, heavy with meaning, it seemed to her. Was the question general, or…? "Do you know him, Captain?"

"I know everyone," he said easily. "I am not such good *ton* as he is, for my father's estate is very modest and I work for a living, but I am accepted in certain less elevated circles of society. I frequent the clubs and gambling houses these aristocratic young men enjoy, and they all come to Tattersall's, where I work. I cannot claim to be a friend of Hesketh's but I am acquainted with him. He is a pleasant man. Very popular in town. No one speaks ill of him."

But… she could hear the word in his tone of voice, see it in his expression, she could almost feel it in the air.

"You know something about him." She made it a statement, not a question, for she was utterly sure. "You know of some reason why I should not marry him."

The Captain and the Country Cousin

For the first time in their acquaintance, the captain looked uncomfortable. "As to whether you should or should not, only you can decide that, Miss Willerton-Forbes. Every man has something detrimental to be said about him — some quirk of his character, some actions in his past that he would not want the world to know. Nor does his wife need to know them, either. Hesketh is a gentleman, a man of honour who pays his debts, does not beat his horses or servants, does not gamble to excess, treats ladies with courtesy. He would make you a good husband."

"But?"

He sighed. "The particular reason he wants to marry you is because you hate London, and never visit. I heard him boasting to his friends that you would not interfere with the mistress he keeps there."

5: *Wives And Mistresses*

It made perfect sense. Mr Hesketh would have his wife in the country and his mistress in the town. Lucinda would be left behind to raise his children, while he would do as he pleased, continuing his indulgent life in London. And it would be Lucinda's fortune which would fund this agreeable life. Her dowry would pay for his mistress.

She felt sick, kicking her horse into unaccustomed speed. Captain Edgerton said nothing more, and they completed their circuit of the park and returned to the stables in silence.

As soon as she thought Lady Morpeth was awake, she went in to her and told her the whole. Lady Morpeth must have gone straight to Lord Morpeth, for Lucinda was called to his dressing room.

"Lucy, this is quite a tale, for he seems such a respectable young man, not at all the sort to— But the aristocracy have different standards from the rest of us, I daresay. It is nothing to them, perfectly normal, in fact."

She had to smile at that. "You are aristocracy yourself, sir."

The Captain and the Country Cousin

"I am still an attorney at heart," he said. "I still *behave* like an attorney, because I have grown up with the idea that the principles under which I was raised are the natural and best ones, and the Scriptures are the best guide. For that reason, I do not like the idea of mistresses. But is it certain? Will you permit me to talk to Wallasey about it? It may be that young Hesketh has changed his ways now that he is considering matrimony."

"Very well, sir."

"There now, give me a kiss and run away, while I see what I may find out."

Lucinda could not bear to be in company when her thoughts were in such turbulence, so she went to her room, throwing open the French doors to breath deeply of the fresh country air. It was illogical, but Hesketh's behaviour seemed to taint it, bringing the faint stench of the Beau Monde's society ways even here, many miles from London.

She was not so prudish as to recoil in horror from male misbehaviour. She knew such things happened, and Wilbraham had a natural daughter from a youthful indiscretion some years before he had married. He had owned his error, the babe and her mother were well cared for, and he had lived a blameless life ever since. Aunt Mary had said only that men were different from women, and sometimes strayed from the path of righteousness, but that did not make them irredeemably wicked.

A mistress was something different, however. That implied an acceptance of such behaviour, not merely an understanding that men were weak but a glorifying of it. To take a woman from her home and family, and keep her purely for the exercise of licentious behaviour was an iniquity which could not be condoned, under any circumstances. She was said to be *'under his protection'*, but what did that mean? That he housed and clothed and fed her, and then discarded her when she was no longer of use to him.

She shivered. To cheer herself up, she opened the drawer where she kept her treasures — the rose and wildflowers, now dried and pressed, the heart-shaped stone and charade, the ribbon from the wild flowers, the lavender cushion and the plum stone. She had enjoyed the hazelnuts, but the bag now contained the last two gingerbread rabbits, which she could not bear to eat.

Carefully laying everything on the bed, touching them, she wondered what it was she wanted in a husband. Not Walter's passionless practicality, that much was certain. She could have married him any time this past four years, if that had been so. But did she want the silent Mr Hesketh, either?

There had been opportunity aplenty to understand his character, during their walks in the garden or half hours pretending to look for books in the library, but she had made no progress. Whatever she asked about — books, music, poetry, the troubles in France, slavery, the prospects for rain — he had no opinion. He read books but could not say what they were about. He heard music every day of his life, but was unable to distinguish one composer from another. He attended the theatre regularly, but knew more of who attended and in which box than the play. She presumed he had undertaken the usual forms of education for a man of his class, but it appeared to have left no impression on his mind.

The Captain and the Country Cousin

He seemed to be as blank a slate as the day he was born. Whatever subject she raised, he would turn aside with a light comment. "Let us not talk about that on such a pleasant day," he would say. Or, "So serious! I cannot think about such matters when I am with you." And that would be the end of it.

She could not say whether his silence would be a soothing aspect of a husband, or whether in time it would irritate her beyond endurance. On one point she was now tolerably certain — that he was not responsible for her pillow gifts. He had not the imagination for it. She had seen not a flicker of romance in him, and she was not sure she could put her life in the hands of such a man.

It was two hours before she was summoned to Lord Morpeth's study. He poured Madeira for her and settled her in one of the big leather chairs beside the fire, taking the other himself.

"Well now, Lucy, I have spoken with Lord Wallasey and with Hesketh, and it is quite true — the boy has a mistress in his keeping. It is usual for young men of rank to do so, and she will be gone before he marries, he tells me. I do not like it, but there it is. They both understand that you have lived a sheltered life, and that you find such matters shocking. Lucy, they would like the opportunity to talk to you… to explain, perhaps, and to persuade you not to turn away from this marriage without careful thought."

"What did you say to that?"

"Why, that it would be up to you, naturally," he said. "You may talk to them or not, as you choose. And if you prefer Hesketh to give up his courtship... if you want him to leave Hurtsmere, he will do as you wish."

"Uncle, what do you think I should do?" Lucinda said. "Do you wish me to marry Mr Hesketh?"

He hesitated. "I would not push you into it if you are the least bit reluctant, niece, but it is a very good match... very eligible on both sides. I do not think you could do better, not without putting yourself through the season and we know your opinion of that. He is the second son of an earl, and although there is no expectation of the title, his father wishes to keep him close and not have him forced into the army. He readily admits he is ill-suited for any other career. Hesketh understands that you prefer to live in the country and hopes that you will establish a loving family home for him. He acknowledges that he has lived an unsettled sort of life and wishes to change that. He admires our family, Lucy, and hopes you will bring him the same sort of happiness, and who could quarrel with such an ambition?"

"Did he say all this himself?" Lucinda said, trying to imagine the taciturn Mr Hesketh expressing himself so articulately.

"Well... he and his father, for they are of one mind on the matter. They are of the opinion that it is too good a match to be undone by such a small detail."

A small detail? Her eyebrows rose at that. That Lord Wallasey and his son should still want the marriage she could understand, but she was surprised that her uncle was so encouraging. "Then you think I should marry him?"

The Captain and the Country Cousin

He sighed. "That choice is entirely yours to make, Lucy. I wish only to ensure that you do not needlessly throw away the best offer you may ever get. After all, when you bury yourself here all the time, the society available to you is severely limited. What are your alternatives? Walter Swinburn? You deserve better."

"Or I could stay here with you and Aunt Mary, and not marry at all."

"Indeed you could, and you will always have a home with us if you want it, my dear, be sure of that, and with Wilbraham after I am gone. We are your family, and will never turn you away. But have you considered what your life will be if you never marry? You are our treasured niece, and Wilbraham's cousin, but with every year that passes, you will be less needed, more dependent. We would not have you give us the best years of your life and dwindle into old age as just another spinster relative, when you could be of the first importance to a family of your own. We want you to be valued as you should be, my dear, as no unmarried woman ever is. So we should like you to consider this offer from Mr Hesketh very carefully."

"Then I will see Lord Wallasey and Mr Hesketh, and hear what they have to say," she said.

They were waiting for her in the library, and as she entered they were standing together in one of the windows. For a moment the two men did not see her and she watched them, fascinated, Lord Wallasey laughing as Mr Hesketh talked animatedly. Lucinda had never seen him so relaxed, so *normal*. If he could only talk to her in that easy way, it would

70

make her decision a great deal easier. Or more difficult, perhaps.

As she closed the door behind her, they became aware of her, and their light-hearted conversation stopped.

"Ah, come in, my dear, come in," Lord Wallasey said, in a hearty manner that she imagined worked very well with invalids and children. Perhaps dogs, too. "Well now, I am sure Morpeth has explained it to you... that you need not trouble yourself about any... entanglements Graham may have, for it will all be dealt with before he marries, you know. All in the past. Nothing at all for you to worry about there. What a young man does when he is single is quite different from what he does when he is married, so you need not give the matter another moment's thought."

Dealt with. That poor woman, enticed into sin and then tossed out of her home at a moment's notice. And what if there were children... One could not so easily sweep them aside. But Lucinda said nothing, for what was there to say?

However, Lord Wallasey was still talking, so she dutifully paid attention to his words... of what a good match it was on both sides. So very suitable, he said. *Suitable.* Such a dispiriting word. But she listened while he enumerated all the benefits of the match, and how well suited they were, and how fortunate Mr Hesketh would be to win her hand. That was rushing on a little too fast for Lucinda, but she could see there was no escaping the proposal now. Somehow, her objection to the mistress, which should have slowed everything down and perhaps halted it altogether, had only managed to bring matters to a head. Here they were, barely a week into what passed for courtship and less than a month after they had first met, possibly on the brink of a betrothal, and she was still not sure whether she wanted to marry Mr Hesketh, or anyone at all.

Lord Wallasey eventually ran out of words. He became hearty again. "Well now, well now... you will not wish to listen to me, I daresay. You wish to hear from Graham. I will leave you two to settle everything between you."

Settle everything! That sounded very final. He was in no doubt of the outcome, then. He left the room, and an awkward silence fell. The longcase clock ticked the seconds away. Mr Hesketh licked his lips, and ran one hand over his breeches.

They were still standing, so Lucinda said, "Shall we sit down, Mr Hesketh?"

There was a pair of chairs set in a niche, not too close to each other, so she took one and waved him to the other. He perched on the very edge of it, and looked as miserable as if he were going to his own execution. She was determined not to speak first, however, so the silence lengthened between them.

He cleared his throat. "So... what do you think?"

Now she was growing impatient. Surely he had some idea of what to say? "About what, Mr Hesketh?" she said crisply.

"Well, about us, obviously. Our marriage. Are you happy now about my—?" He broke off in confusion.

"Your mistress? Tell me, do you consider it acceptable for a man to have a mistress?"

The Captain and the Country Cousin

"Of course!" He looked puzzled. "Father has explained all that. It is perfectly normal. Everyone does it, but if it shocks you—"

"It does not shock me, sir. I am not so out of the world that I know nothing of society. It does disquiet me, however, as it should you also. *'For this is the will of God, even your sanctification, that ye should abstain from fornication.'* Or do you not follow the teachings of the Holy Book? You should, or your immortal soul may be at risk."

He flushed, but she thought he was angry rather than embarrassed. "You are very free with your opinions, madam."

"Mr Hesketh, we are discussing the possibility of a marriage between us, and in order to make a decision on that point, I must understand your character. It is necessary to be perfectly sure that you are a man who may be respected and esteemed, who will guide his wife and children in the proper path. A man of good principles. At this moment, I cannot say that of you with any certainty."

"And I cannot say that you are a woman who will bring me any comfort in my life, if you are set to nag me with these sanctimonious prosings. That is not what a man wants when he goes home, I can tell you that much. Good Lord, you want a saint as a husband, and I regret that I am only human. You are a fool if you throw away what may be the best offer you will ever have. I can go to town and find myself half a dozen women with better rank and better fortunes than yours, yes, and better looks, too. Not that you are an antidote, but still..."

Well, he could be articulate after all, when he was berating her. Sanctimonious prosings, indeed! "Why, I thank you for the compliment, sir." She laughed, her spirits rising, but that seemed to incense him even more.

"Half a dozen or more, I tell you. I could have married a score of times, had I wished it, but I want to oblige Father and you *seem* like—"

"Such a country mouse?" she said sweetly.

"Well, yes, if you must have the truth. You would suit me perfectly, and we were going on so well before. Devil take whoever told you about my mistress, and turned you against me."

"It is not the mere fact that you have a mistress that distresses me," she said more gently, "but that you planned to leave me in the country while keeping your mistress in town."

"That is a foul lie!"

She stared at him in astonishment. "Are you calling Captain Edgerton a liar?"

"Edgerton? What business is it of his, I might wonder?"

"He knows you and so I asked for his opinion of you," she said.

"The devil you did! You have been against me right from the start, then, just looking for something about me of which you can disapprove. Are you happy now? You can be as supercilious as you like now that you have discovered that I am mortal, like other men. If you are holding out for perfection, you will surely die an old maid. You can have rank and fortune and a position in society, and I will be a good husband to you, Lucinda. I can be generous, to those who behave sensibly towards me but this... this *shrewishness* will not do at all. I shall not stand for it when we are married, and so I warn you."

"How kind of you, to offer me a rank only slightly higher than my own, and a position in society, which I do not want. How reassuring that you will be generous when you have my dowry in your hand. Will you use my own money to buy presents for me, or to make improvements to my own house? Your philanthropy knows no bounds. Mr Hesketh, may I remind you that you have not yet offered for me, and I have not yet accepted you."

"What is this about, if you are not going to accept? Have you kept me dangling all this time, and with no intention of going through with it? You are a jilt, Lucinda, and I am not sure I want *you*, after all this."

She rose to her feet, obliging him to rise also, anger rising up to choke her. "Then we are at a stand, and can have nothing further to say to each other, Mr Hesketh." He exhaled sharply, reddening. She was heartily sick of him, but having achieved her freedom, she was minded to be magnanimous. Holding out her hand, she said, "Come, let us part as friends. You are much better off without me, you know. We would have ended by hating each other, and this way we both have the opportunity to find someone better suited."

For a moment he glared at her, but then perhaps good breeding reasserted itself and he shook her hand. With a bow, he turned and stalked out of the room.

Lucinda laughed in sheer exhilaration. She had not realised until that moment how little she had relished the prospect of this marriage. Perhaps, as Captain Edgerton had said, she had been looking for a reason to evade it.

She could not help remembering her own words to Lavinia. *'I would marry tomorrow if I could only find a man who inspires my affection. More than that — I want a man who excites me, someone with whom I could spend my whole life and not be bored. And where am I to find such a man?'*

Where, indeed?

6: *The Long Gallery*

Dinner that day was a more fraught affair than usual, although not because anyone displayed anger or dismay. On the contrary, everyone was conspicuously pretending that nothing at all had happened, and Mr Hesketh was still amongst the guests, for heaven forbid that he should create a scandal by leaving with unseemly haste. The ladies were a little frigid, for Lucinda was displaying her rustic manners by objecting to a mistress. A well-bred lady would pretend to know nothing at all about such matters. However, there was a surprising degree of solicitude shown to Lucinda by the gentlemen, as though they were trying to outdo each other in courtesy in order to prove that they bore her no ill-will for disrupting their carefully concocted plans. Fortunately, there were still a few guests from outside the two families who behaved exactly as usual.

One of them was Captain Edgerton, and Lucinda blessed his easy manner, and his bottomless well of entertaining stories. His section of the table seemed to be in constant gales of laughter, while the Dowager Countess of Wallasey, her face wreathed in a most unaccustomed smile, tapped him archly on the hand with her spoon, and said, "Really, sir, what a Banbury tale!"

Lucinda was relieved of the company of Mr Hesketh at last, which gave her ample opportunity to determine that she could not regret her actions. Now that the threat of a proposal was removed, she felt positively light-hearted. Her only sorrow was that there would be no more little pillow gifts now.

After dinner, she was soon summoned to the pianoforte again, while some of the younger members of the party got up an impromptu dance. She felt she ought to mind being relegated to the ranks of matrons and chaperons, for she was only twenty-four, after all, and young enough to dance herself if she wished. But she did not wish. It suited her very well to hide behind the instrument, while Titus danced with one young lady after another. He seemed disinclined to make a choice of bride, but he revelled in the attention.

She was not unnoticed in her hiding place, however, for Captain Edgerton brought her tea to her, and stayed to talk for a little while. Even when she began playing again, he stood beside her, humming along to the tune, his foot tapping, and his cheerful spirits, as always, made her smile.

But then one of the Hesketh girls came to beg him to dance, and she was left alone again.

That night, she went to her chamber without any expectations, but there on the pillow was a small bunch of Michaelmas daisies. So her admirer was *not* Graham Hesketh after all. Now she had to begin her puzzling all over again. Her suitor, whoever he was, must have been in the castle at the time of the red rose, must still be at the castle, and must have gone on the riding expedition, which had called at the bakery famous for its gingerbread.

She quickly narrowed her list to four possible suspects — one or other of the younger Hesketh brothers, one or other of the Hartridge brothers, Captain Edgerton, or some other person who was merely teasing her. If the latter, it could be anyone, but she could think of no one who would inflict such a cruel joke on her. And as for the others, none of them had shown the least sign of admiration in reality. The captain was very ready with a compliment, but that was just his flirtatious nature, meaning precisely nothing. Since he had told her himself that he was not looking for a wife, she could not believe that he would go to the trouble of picking locks to leave flowers for her. She could not believe that *anyone* would do such a thing unless they wished to secure her affections, and if that were so, staying anonymous was pointless.

She gave it up, and determined that she would enjoy her little gifts while they lasted, but waste no more time trying to interpret them.

~~~~~

As if the very sky had decided that it had tired of summer and was ready for autumn, the next day was wet. A steady downpour set the drainpipes gurgling and washed away the view from the windows in a rainy haze.

The wet weather decreed that there was nothing for the castle's residents to do but stay indoors, and find enough occupation in books or sketchbooks or journals or games of one sort or another. The older guests settled down with pleasure to an unexpected daytime session at the card tables, while the younger ones pulled out volumes of Shakespeare and read stirring or tragic or romantic passages, as best appealed to them.

Lucinda was not minded for Shakespeare of any variety, and she was not needed by the three countesses or the housekeeper, so she decided to go to the Long Gallery to get some exercise.

She was not the first to have that idea. At the far end of the gallery, a coatless Captain Edgerton was hefting a sword. His back was to her as he paced about, slashing back and forth at some imaginary enemy. Two footmen manning the ladder used to retrieve the sword stood watching, mesmerised.

Lucinda was mesmerised too. She had grown up in a family of attorneys, not military men. There were a couple of pistols kept in a locked cabinet somewhere, in case of intrusion or other emergency, but until she moved to Hurtsmere Castle she had never even seen a sword, and this was the first time that anyone had bothered to take any of them down from the wall.

The captain's movements brought him round to face Lucinda, but he was so intent on his invisible enemy that at first he did not notice her. When he did, his face was lit by a warm smile, and as always, she could not help herself from smiling back at him. No one could be downhearted when the captain was there.

The Captain and the Country Cousin

"I am glad you have found an opportunity to examine our swords more closely, Captain. What do you think of them so far?"

"This is such a fine collection, Miss Willerton-Forbes," he said, walking towards her. "So many interesting examples. This one I have been trying is of a type that might have been used in the Crusades — in a battle of that era, anyway. One uses both hands to wield it, like this, you see?" He raised it and made a downward slash. "It is a little blunt now, but in its prime it would have cut right through chain mail."

"Is it heavy?"

"Try it." Coming up to her with a grin, he shifted the sword so that it lay on his arm, with the hilt towards her.

"Oh... may I?"

"You will need both hands."

Gingerly she placed her hands around the hilt and lifted. "Oh! It is not as heavy as I supposed."

His smile widened. "I was surprised, too. It is very long — too long for me, in truth — but the solidity of it makes one imagine it must be heavy. But when one considers the matter, the need for a swordsman to wield his weapon perhaps for hours at a time dictates the lightest weight compatible with its function."

"I can see that," she said. "How should I hold it? Like this? And then move it like this, as you were doing? Oh, it feels quite comfortable, but it is as you say, such a device needs to be easy to use."

The Captain and the Country Cousin

"It still requires a great deal of practice to become adept with it. Now this one here is interesting. It is designed to be used with only one hand and just a touch of the fingers of the other. A most unusual sword. This pair above the fireplace is probably from the Civil War. That basket-shaped hilt is very distinctive. Will you try that one? John, put the broadsword back, will you, and fetch down that one there. Yes, that one."

"That is a little lighter," she said. "Is it used the same way? Like this?" She swished it about in the air.

"It can be," he said. "Those with long, wide blades used with both hands are designed for slashing alone. This one can also be used to stab your enemy in the heart, like so. And a rapier is designed principally for stabbing. It depends on the kind of fight one is facing. On an open battlefield, a long, slashing sword is most useful. At closer quarters, something shorter is better, like that cutlass there."

She heard him in fascination. "There is an art even to killing," she said quietly.

His smile faded. "Not to killing, no. In a battle, survival is all that matters, and there is not much art to that. Skill, perhaps. Training and trust in one's comrades and belief in the rightness of the cause, certainly. But a fair amount of luck, too."

"But there is art in the making of these weapons," she said, pointing to two elegant examples still on the wall. "This pair, for instance. The metalwork is exquisite."

"Spanish, I think," he said, the smile back almost instantaneously. "Duelling rapiers. John, would you please…? Thank you. Careful! They look very sharp, still. Now these are much lighter, you see." He handed her one by the hilt, as before. "Perfect for a duel, and also to carry in the street, to deter pickpockets, although there is less need these days."

She swished it about thoughtfully. "The sword you wore when you arrived — is that a rapier?"

"A little more solid than that — a smallsword, as it is called. I like something with a bit of weight, and a bit shorter than these, being on the short side myself. But these duelling rapiers are wonderfully light."

She was thrilled at his openness, and ventured to ask a more personal question. "Have you ever been in a duel, Captain?"

He shook his head. "Duelling is for fools."

"Nonsense, Edgerton," came a voice from behind them. "Duelling is for *gentlemen.*"

They spun round, the rapiers still in their hands, to see Graham Hesketh, his lips curled into a sneer. Behind him, still arriving, a crowd of the younger members of the party, obviously engaged on a tour of the building.

Captain Edgerton bowed punctiliously. "Hesketh, ladies, gentlemen. How delightful of you to join us. But if you are correct, Hesketh, then I am happy not to be a gentlemen."

Mr Hesketh's sneer broadened. "And swords are for gentlemen, also," he said, turning his supercilious eye on Lucinda. "What are you about, Edgerton, to be allowing Miss Willerton-Forbes to handle a sword? Give it to me, my dear, before you hurt yourself."

The Captain and the Country Cousin

He strode across to her, reaching out his hand. His peremptory tone was intensely irritating. Without thinking, she raised the tip of the blade so it pointed at his throat, and he had to stop dead to avoid being spiked by it. "You are the one at the sharp end, Mr Hesketh," she said coolly.

Someone sniggered, and Mr Hesketh glared at her, but dared not say anything more.

Into the silence that fell, one of the Hartridge sons coughed cautiously. "How then would you settle matters of honour without duelling, Edgerton?"

"With an apology, offered and accepted," the captain said at once, not at all dismayed by the question. "An honourable man should be able to admit to his mistake, and set it right, if he can. No one should die because of words spoken in anger, or hasty actions, soon regretted."

"Would you never accept a challenge?" Mr Hesketh said. "Some would call it cowardly to refuse."

Lucinda was not much accustomed to male tensions, for the Willerton-Forbes men were peaceable creatures, but she was aware of a certain edginess in the air, as if some quite different conversation were going on beneath the politely-worded surface. It was like the heaviness before a summer storm.

Captain Edgerton looked at Mr Hesketh thoughtfully, as if weighing his words, "I cannot say that I would *never* accept a challenge of honour. Perhaps if there were no other option available, but I like to think that I would find alternative solutions, something milder than a fight to the death. I have done my share of killing, and have no wish to repeat the experience."

"Something milder?" Mr Hesketh said. "What say you to a fencing match? You are an expert on swords, so I daresay you would fancy your chances, and we have the rapiers to hand, if I can prise this one from Miss Willerton-Forbes' hand."

The captain raised his eyebrows. "Against you? Then let it be so, Hesketh. If we tip the blades with slivers of cork, we should not do too much damage to each other."

One of the footmen was dispatched to the kitchen to find cork, Lucinda's blade was handed over to Mr Hesketh and the two men stripped down to their shirts, sleeves rolled up. A few small items of furniture and breakable ornaments were moved to safer quarters. Some of the gentlemen wondered aloud if the ladies really wished to watch a sword fight, and a chaperon shooed her charges away, but most waited, fascinated and horrified in equal measure. Sword fights were a male preserve, and ladies were rarely afforded a glimpse of such activities.

Lucinda did not leave. Part of her was curious to see the rapiers used... not in anger, she hoped, but as they were intended to be used. Much as she had enjoyed her conversation with Captain Edgerton and trying the swords for herself, it was that initial moment that hung in her memory. When she had entered the Long Gallery, she had been held spellbound to see him wielding a sword almost as tall as he was, just as if he were in battle in the Middle Ages, a Crusader in the Holy Land, fighting for God and his country. The rapiers were not quite such impressive weapons, but she very much wanted to see them in action. No... if she were honest, what she truly wanted was to see Captain Edgerton in action again. She had no desire at all to see Graham Hesketh fighting. He was strutting around, laughing with his friends, every inch exuding self-confidence. He was a head taller than his opponent, after all. But if she were a gambler, she would have put all her money on Captain Edgerton, waiting quietly, one shoulder leaning against the wall.

The footman returned with the cork, and the captain carefully cut pieces to protect the tips of the blades. Then the two men saluted each other, swords raised, and the fight began. At first Mr Hesketh danced around, lunging with his sword then jumping back again, while the captain stood, not quite motionless, but taking only a single step here, then standing, then another step. It made her think of backgammon, one player making a running game, racing round the board, the other piling up pieces in defence. But then the captain moved, lightning fast, and there was a brief flurry of action, too fast for Lucinda to see.

"A hit!" called out one of the Hartridges.

Mr Hesketh grunted in acknowledgement and the two swordsmen parted, raised their swords, began again. The second hit took longer to achieve, but again it was the captain who succeeded. It was at that point that something changed, some indefinable quality of the atmosphere, and the game became deadly serious. It was not Captain Edgerton who changed, of that she was sure, for he had the same posture throughout, alert, steady, intent on his opponent, with no thought of those watching. No, it was Mr Hesketh who shifted from a light-hearted attitude, showing off a little, playing for the audience, to a much more intense stance. Now he was truly fighting.

There was something terrifying in the fierceness of the two men, their eyes locked on each other. They both desperately wanted to win, and all their focus was on that, every muscle engaged to that end, their concentration absolute. Lucinda found she was holding her breath. To her surprise, she was not at all an impartial observer. She knew exactly who she wanted to win.

A long, quick-moving bout, both men as light on their feet as cats, brought about a violent clash of steel on steel, a yell from Mr Hesketh and "A hit! Well done," from Captain Edgerton. But this time, they did not move apart and the two clashed again and again. Now the captain was moving forward, pressing his opponent. Another hit! He moved back, but Mr Hesketh lunged wildly at him and there was another crashing of sword against sword.

Something flew through the air — a piece of cork!

"Graham!" an urgent voice called out, but there was no stopping Hesketh. Had he not realised? Or did he simply not care, the desire to win overwhelming all good sense?

A spasm of pure fear shot through Lucinda. Captain Edgerton was entirely at his opponent's mercy now, and the slightest mistake would see him hurt... he could be killed! She had a sudden vision of him lying on the ground, motionless, blood streaming out of him unstoppably. No! He must not die, he must *not!*

Hesketh pressed forward. Captain Edgerton danced out of range, but his opponent followed, lunging at him again and again. There were more voices calling, but he did not seem to hear. Again the captain retreated, parrying thrust after thrust, then, abruptly, he dropped to one knee, sliding sideways, and with his free hand caught Mr Hesketh behind the knees, so that he came crashing to the ground, his rapier flying from his hand. The captain was on his feet again instantly, his sword at the fallen man's throat.

"Enough," he said gruffly.

The silence was broken only by the heavy breathing of the two swordsmen.

Then, shakily, Mr Hesketh huffed a breath, and held up his hands. "Have it your way, Edgerton. Lord, did I pink you?" Then he laughed.

"The tip fell from your blade," the captain said, turning away.

That was when Lucinda saw the bright red stain on his shirt.

7: The Housekeeper's Room

Captain Edgerton moved away to hand his sword to one of the footmen and collect his waistcoat and coat. Lucinda ran after him, her eye fixed on the red stain on his left upper arm. Was it still spreading? She thought it was.

"You are hurt!"

He smiled, as if nothing were amiss. "It is the merest scratch."

"Come down to the housekeeper's room, and let me see to it for you."

He shook his head. "My man will deal with it. He is used to patching me up."

"Your groom may be the best surgeon in the world, Captain, but while you are a guest in my house, you will allow me to attend to such matters."

He bowed in acquiescence, and without a glance at Mr Hesketh, he headed for the stairs.

"Not that way," she said. "Better not walk down the main stairs so informally attired, and bleeding, too. You may enjoy one of our multitude of spiral staircases."

Laughing, he followed her, and she lifted the tapestry that hid the door to the stair. He exclaimed with delight at this secret, and as they descended, he ran his hands appreciatively over the stone walls and admired the tightness of the spiral.

"Most impractical," Lucinda said. "Impossible even for the servants to carry a tray up and down. I cannot imagine what the architect was thinking."

"But so defensible," the captain said. "One swordsman could hold an entire army at bay. Sadly, there is seldom a need for such measures these days. I was born several hundred years too late."

"You would have enjoyed the Middle Ages, would you?" she said, amused.

"Oh, probably not. Dashed uncomfortable, I suspect, what with all the fleas and mud, and no decent linen or port. But they had some glorious battles, which I would like to have seen. Agincourt. Tours. Bosworth. Hastings. Marston Moor. So fascinating to watch."

"From a safe distance, I hope."

"But that would be no fun at all," he said, making her laugh.

The housekeeper's room was empty, Mrs Philips presumably having been called to some far-flung corner of her domain. Lucinda could not suppress a feeling of glee to have the captain to herself. Of all the castle's current crop of guests, he was the only one whom she felt a desire to know better. A rather strong desire at that moment, to be truthful.

"Sit down here, Captain, and remove your shirt."

She brought a wooden chair closer to a small table covered with an embroidered cloth.

"Miss Willerton-Forbes, I cannot think that this is appropriate. I am quite happy for the housekeeper to physick me, if you insist, but it is hardly fitting for you to do it."

"Shirt off," she said crisply. "I shall just fetch some warm water."

When she came back, bowl in hand, he had released the injured arm from its sleeve, but the rest of him was chastely covered. It was probably just as well, for the sight of just one arm of well-honed male flesh with its full complement of muscles made her quiver. A little water slopped out of the bowl.

"Can you manage?" he said solicitously.

Momentarily unable to speak, she nodded, and hastily set the bowl down on the table. Rummaging through cupboards and drawers for cloths and ointment put him out of her sight briefly, and allowed her to regain her composure. Then she damped a cloth in the water, and set to work, head down, avoiding his eyes. She could feel herself blushing, and at her age, too! How missish of her.

With the blood cleaned away, she could see that it was, as he had said, only a scratch. Still, it was as well to have it properly cleaned and bound. Such an intimate moment! She

The Captain and the Country Cousin

had bandaged a thousand wounds, nursed any number of invalids, had mended her uncle and several of her cousins when they fell from ladders, or stabbed themselves with pruning knives, or in one case was trodden on by a horse. But she had never before tended to a man who exuded masculinity in a way that she could barely understand.

He made no sound as she worked on the wound, even when she washed it with alcohol. The silence was beginning to make her feel uncomfortable, so she said in a cheerful tone, "If you like war so well, I wonder you do not sign up with the regulars, Captain. There is plenty of fighting to be had these days."

She had expected a flippant answer, but to her surprise he said, "I may joke about it, but war is a dreadful business, Miss Willerton-Forbes. I have seen my share of misery and want no more of it. Men enter into it lightly, looking for adventure or glory or riches or trying to forget, or death, sometimes, or just to get away from home and be a man at last. And they find only blood and pain and unspeakable horrors. There is no hell on earth more desperate than the field of battle after all is over. The screams of men and horses, the smell of gunpowder in the air, the mud everywhere. So many good men cut down in their youth, all their potential wiped out by one stray cannonball or unlucky sword. They will never write poetry again, never see their mother's smile, never drink and wench and wager with their friends, never fall in love. I am finished with war. If ever Boney gets across the Channel, naturally I shall play my part to chase him back to France, but until then, I am content to wield my sword for sport, not survival."

The Captain and the Country Cousin

So serious! She could not answer his heartfelt words, but the last point was one she could address. Whatever had happened in the Long Gallery, it was not mere sport. "It was hard to tell the difference between sport and survival just now. You could have been killed."

He smiled a little, his eyes gleaming with amusement. "No, no, I was never at serious risk, I assure you. I am very sorry if you were alarmed by what you saw."

"I was, for a moment, but you dealt with him very speedily. Until that point, I was enjoying the contest very well, although..." There it was again, that question of masculinity that she could not even articulate. She lowered her gaze again, concentrating on the salve she was applying to the wound.

"Although?"

"I have never seen a sword fight before, and I know that a duel is a very serious matter. But this was not a duel, so I supposed that, being just a game, it would be light-hearted... that there would be jesting between you, and fun, and it did not look like fun at all. It seemed very serious."

"A game of any sort is only fun if one does not mind whether one wins or loses," he said. "And what is the point of playing unless one tries to win?"

"Do you always play to win?"

"Always. If I feel the game is impossible to win, I do not play at all. Most men are the same — competitive. Is it not the same for you?"

"Not at all. I play spillikins to amuse the children. I play cribbage with the Dowager Countess because no one else wants to be shouted at. I play whist when Lady Morpeth needs me to make up a four."

He shook his head. "Everything you do is for other people. Do you never do anything for your own pleasure?"

"Frequently, sir. I am not a slave, or a paid companion. I am treated as a daughter of the house, and have always been so. It gives me a great deal of pleasure to repay my aunt and uncle for their kindness, but I am free to pursue my own interests whenever I wish to."

"And how often do you wish to?"

That made her raise her eyes again. He was smiling at her, his whole face alight with amusement, but also sympathy. She blushed again under his scrutiny, but sat back a little to answer him. "You mistake me, Captain Edgerton, if you imagine me to be deferring my own pleasures for the sake of my relations. My ministrations are not solely on their account, I assure you. My greatest joy, you see, is to be organising. People, households, excursions, shopping trips, wardrobes… it matters not, to me. Lady Morpeth's kindly nature leads her to encourage me in the habit—"

"She takes advantage of you."

"We take advantage of each other, I assure you. She likes to write long, chatty letters to far-flung friends and relations—"

"And sleep on the sofa," he said, his eyes twinkling in a way that made her stomach flutter in the most peculiar way.

The Captain and the Country Cousin

"She tires easily," Lucinda said, with mock severity. "And although she enjoys company, she is not very good at the social obligations, so I suggest people she might care to invite for dinner or to take tea with us of an evening or to enjoy a visit to the garden, and she writes to invite them. That way, she has interesting society, and Uncle Quentin is assured of suitable whist partners. But if there is one thing I adore, it is arranging entertainments on a large scale. I have been in heaven these past few weeks, I assure you, and I would have taken it very ill if Aunt Mary had attempted to interfere with my plans."

"Do the other countesses take this in good part?"

She laughed suddenly. "Oh, the three of them are so funny! They are all so very correct, trying very hard not to step on each other's toes. The Dowager and the Young Countess are too polite to interfere in any way with how Aunt Mary runs the castle, and she is terrified of upsetting them by changing things. If I had not taken charge, nothing at all would ever have been done. How they would go on without me I cannot imagine. No, that is not quite true. The Young Countess would whistle up an indigent relative or two. They had it all planned out between them, if I should—"

"Marry?" he said softly.

She nodded, but since she had no wish to talk about Mr Hesketh, she reached in silence for a bandage and began to bind his arm.

There was a rumble of male voices outside, then the door burst open and a gaggle of them burst in — Mr Hesketh, with Titus and several other Heskeths and a couple of

Hartridges, and the room seemed unbearably crowded, suddenly.

"Well, Edgerton, I came to see how you are doing," Mr Hesketh said. "Not at death's door, I see."

"No need for the black coats this time," the captain said easily. "I am sorry our match ended so abruptly, however. I was enjoying it very much."

There was a long silence, as one or two people shuffled their feet. Hesketh looked conscious, but he said stiffly, "The fault was mine. I did not notice that the cork protector had fallen off."

"Easily done in the heat of battle," Edgerton said, with his ready smile. "No harm done. Perhaps we might continue our match another time? I fear I am *hors de combat* for a while, but perhaps when we are both in town. Do you ever go to Angelo's? I fence there sometimes."

"I shall look forward to it. Glad you are not seriously injured, Edgerton. No hard feelings, eh?"

He held out his hand, and the captain shook it. "None at all."

"Good. Very good," Hesketh said. "Well, we shall leave you to the ministrations of your nurse." So saying, they all turned and squeezed out of the door. Their voices could be heard laughing and joking together, gradually fading into the distance.

"There, that is done," Lucinda said, knotting the ends of the bandage.

The Captain and the Country Cousin

Captain Edgerton slid his arm into the empty sleeve of his shirt, and she was afforded a brief glimpse of his well-muscled chest, so distracting that she was obliged to avert her eyes. "I thank you, Miss Willerton-Forbes. That was gently done."

"Let me know if it bleeds again."

"I shall do so." After a pause, he went on, "You must not mind all this male posturing. He is upset with me because I scuppered his plan to wed you, that is all, and when men become upset, they fight. He will recover."

"He sank his own plans by keeping a mistress and expecting me not to mind," she said acidly.

The captain laughed and shook his head. "Any lady would mind, but most would not have the courage to say so."

"Everyone tells me that it is *normal* to keep a mistress," she said fretfully. "I cannot believe it!"

He frowned, then said, "For those born into the nobility, marriages are a matter of practicality."

"Suitability!" she said, with such obvious distaste that he laughed out loud.

"Exactly so! Those in such a position must hope for affection, but settle for civility. Friendship, perhaps. In such cases, a man may feel himself entitled to look for affection elsewhere."

This aspect to the matter had not previously occurred to Lucinda. "So Mr Hesketh might be in love with his mistress? Perhaps that is why he does not wish to throw her over. His father wishes him to help secure the succession by having sons, and he is willing to oblige, but he wants to keep his mistress too."

Captain Edgerton looked wary. "It is possible."

"And I unhelpfully threw his careful plans into disarray! Oh dear. I can see that there is more to this than I had considered. But still, are mistresses so common?"

"It is quite a widespread practice. Men... most men enjoy the company of women, are drawn to them very strongly. It is a very powerful and primeval attraction that is impossible to ignore. A gentleman cannot act on that kind of attraction with a lady, so sometimes, if he has no wife to turn to, he looks elsewhere. A mistress is one solution to that problem."

"Is it so? Then perhaps it truly is normal. Do *you*—? Oh, I beg your pardon, that is unforgivably rude."

He laughed, but a little uneasily. "I invited the question, did I not? I have never had a mistress, not even in India, where it is a very common practice." Then he smiled, his eyes twinkling, and leaned forward to whisper conspiratorially. "That does not mean I have lived like a monk, however."

For a moment she did not catch his meaning, but when she did, she blushed hotly, hands to cheeks. "Oh! I did not— Captain, I— Oh, my goodness!"

He laughed again, more readily this time. "We are having such an open conversation, Miss Willerton-Forbes, that I could not resist. However, this is all most improper. We should not be discussing such a subject at all."

"No, of course not," she said, smiling a little ruefully. "You are so easy to talk to that I was quite led astray. But it

The Captain and the Country Cousin

has been most informative. I do feel it is the sort of subject that a young lady ought to discuss, the better to understand the men she encounters. I am very grateful to you, sir, for alerting me to Mr Hesketh's situation. I think I should have been dreadfully unhappy with him."

"I should not have spoken about it to you," he said, with a sudden frown. "I broke his confidence and he was quite right to confront me over it. That was why I accepted his challenge, because I knew I was in the wrong. But I could not stand silently by and watch you walk into that marriage with your eyes closed, unaware of his character." His tone hardened, becoming unexpectedly savage. "You deserve better than him, a great deal better. In fact, I am not sure that *anyone* is worthy of you."

And with a bow, he was gone, leaving Lucinda bewildered by his forceful words, but hopeful, too. For surely he could not speak so unless he felt some affection for her? Was he her mystery suitor? She felt a frisson of excitement at the thought.

What was happening to her? When she had entered the Long Gallery just a short time ago, she had certainly *liked* Captain Edgerton well enough, for he was by far the most interesting man she had ever met. He was not dull like Walter Swinburn, or selfish like Graham Hesketh. Nor was he gently ordinary, like the Willerton-Forbes men. He was honourable and gallant and well-mannered, but he was also dangerously attractive. She admired his concentration when he had a sword in his hand, the elegant economy of his movements as he fought, his fine physique — yes, particularly that. No one like him had even crossed her path before, and she was very much afraid she was falling in love with him, with a man who had made it plain he was not in want of a wife.

Was it possible that he was responsible for her pillow gifts? If so, surely they had now reached a point where he might begin to court her openly. So far, he had treated her with the utmost courtesy, but had not singled her out at all, and most of their meetings had been by chance. If he cared at all, then surely after the intimacy of the time spent in the housekeeper's room he would begin to show his hand. Perhaps even tonight...

But he did not. Indeed, far from paying her more attention, it almost seemed as if he were avoiding her. They exchanged not a single word all evening, and he never came within earshot, so she had not even the pleasure of hearing his voice.

Lucinda went to her bedchamber on the verge of tears. Why? Why would he say no one was worthy of her and speak with such passion, yet not even ask her how she did, or pay her some meaningless compliment? Confusing man!

But her pillow brought her its nightly comfort. A slip of paper rested on it, with another charade.

'Before a circle let appear,

Twice twenty-five and five in rear;

One fifth of eight subjoin and then

You'll quickly find what conquers man.'

This one was much easier to solve. Two minutes with pencil and paper brought her the answer: *'LOVE'*. A declaration indeed! If Captain Edgerton had failed her, then her mystery suitor had not, and was courting her even more determinedly.

But who was it?

~~~~~

For three more days the castle echoed to girlish laughter and music and deep-voiced male conversation. There was one last riding party, in which Lucinda took part, a palm-reading by a Romany woman, and a theatrical evening, consisting of readings from plays and recitations of poems and a pretend battle between the Montagues and Capulets, although with wooden swords. A final grand dinner was held for a number of local families. Tomorrow the last of the guests would leave, the three countesses would sink back with relief into their somnolence, and Lucinda would once more test her ingenuity in securing whist players of Lord Morpeth's standard.

And still her secret admirer had not spoken. But there on the pillow that night was a single red rose again, and this time there was a paper tucked beneath it, inscribed with the now familiar strong hand.

'My love is like a red, red rose

That's newly sprung in June

My love is like a melody

So sweetly played in tune.'

No charade this time, no pretence, no obfuscation — a simple declaration of love. Lucinda hugged it to her breast, thrilled to have such proof of ardour.

Surely now he would speak?

8: Waiting

Lucinda dressed with unusual care the next morning, choosing one of her newest dresses, barely worn. She threaded the stone heart onto a ribbon and tied it around her neck. If her lover were shy, perhaps that would give him a little push in the right direction. Although it had not worked before, she had to admit.

She was in a strange, dithery mood, aware that Captain Edgerton had awoken feelings in her that she had never experienced before. She lay awake at night storing up little memories — his smile with the amused eyes, his intensity with a sword, the way he joked and entertained with his stories, the way the muscles moved in his arm... Lord, she was in such danger with him! It was her misfortune that he was not looking for a wife, and he had never given her the slightest hint of regard for her.

Then there was her mysterious suitor. There, if she wanted it, was evidence of regard, with roses and poems and talk of admiration and love. But what did it mean? Was someone sporting with her feelings? She could not bear to think so. Surely he would give her some sign before he left the castle?

But as the morning wore away, and carriage after carriage drew up before the door, was loaded with luggage and smiling passengers, and rolled away down the drive, no sign was forthcoming. Mr Hesketh and his younger brothers left early, bound for a shooting party in Norfolk. The Hartridges departed in a noisy gaggle, with several carriages and riders. Even Aunt Guinevere was well enough to make the journey home, in an imposing procession of three carriages and two outriders.

Captain Edgerton left too, a quieter departure, just himself and his groom on horseback, but his value as a guest was clear, for both Lord and Lady Morpeth were in the entrance hall to bid him farewell.

"Come and visit us again whenever you like," Lord Morpeth said. "No need to wait for Pettigrew, for you might wait forever."

"I cannot say when I might next be spared from my work," the captain said. "Perhaps we will all have the good fortune to meet in town before too long, and I might have an opportunity to recoup some of my card table losses? I do not usually go down so deeply, and would like my revenge, my lord."

"Lady Morpeth and I will be there when Parliament sits, and you are welcome to try your luck again," Lord Morpeth said, chuckling. "Do not expect to see Luce, however, for she hates the place."

The Captain and the Country Cousin

"I am sorry to hear that," he said politely, without any attempt to cajole or tease her. She could not suppress her disappointment.

Within a very few moments, he had leapt onto his horse with an agility that made her sigh, and was trotting off down the drive. Lucinda was very sorry to see him leave, not only for her own sake, in losing someone she had come to look upon as a friend, but because he had lifted everyone's spirits so wonderfully. Still, it was surely for the best. Since she had nothing to hope or expect from him, it was better that she saw him no more.

The last to leave was Everard, with Lady Jane Hesketh and Lord and Lady Wallasey. They were bound for one of the earl's smaller estates, which would be the young couple's home after they were wed, for heaven forbid an earl's daughter should live above an attorney's office, as Everard had done.

The doors closed for the last time, and Lucinda returned to the Great Hall, where a battered old table was laden with cut blooms and vases for her to arrange. Titus followed her there, and stood wreathed in gloom, idly kicking one leg of the table.

"What will you do without Everard?" Lucinda said gently.

"Cannot imagine," Titus said, looking up with a rueful smile. "We have barely been separated for a day in thirty-five years, except for that time he broke his leg at Eton. Oh, and when I had measles and he did not. But otherwise, we have done everything together. And now I shall go back to being an attorney, and he will move up in the world and our paths will seldom cross, I expect," he ended disconsolately.

"He will visit here all the time, never fear, and you will go there," she said. "He will not forget his twin just because he is married. But how about your plans? Did you find any of the young ladies to your liking?"

"All of them," he said, laughing. "They are all very agreeable, pleasant girls, but... well, it never moved to the next stage. I never felt inclined to *talk* to any of them."

Lucinda paused, a tall gladiolus stem poised in mid-air. "To talk to them? Do you not talk to them anyway?"

"Oh, yes, of course," Titus said. "One talks, but about trivial things — did she enjoy the ball, is she going to the library, does she like riding, the weather. So much about the weather! And the little compliments — what a fetching bonnet, Miss Smith, the ribbon exactly matches your eyes, that sort of thing. It pleases them, but it means nothing. Everybody knows it means nothing, so a fellow is safe, you see? There is that barrier of politeness between a man and a woman, so he is protected. But once that barrier begins to crumble, why then anything may happen. I knew precisely the moment Everard began to fall in love with Jane, because he started talking about clouds."

"Clouds?" she said, laughing.

Titus laughed too. "I know, it sounds crazy, does it not? We were walking in one of the parks — Hyde Park, probably. Everard was with Jane and I was with... oh, the girl with red hair, I forget her name, and the chaperons were behind us. It was one of those days when the clouds were just scudding overhead, shifting and changing shape the whole time, and Everard pointed up to a cloud and said, '*Look at that — a donkey.*' And Jane was talking the same way, seeing castles and waves and stairs — stairs! I ask you! They might have been talking in Chinese for all I understood of it. We reached a lake of some sort and the rest of us were admiring the trees, which were just in leaf then and very pretty, but Everard and Jane were not even looking, they were engrossed in some conversation about ships and travelling and the infinite majesty of the ocean, and I knew then that he was smitten. Once a fellow starts talking that way to a girl, about *real* things, deep things, he is lost. He has exposed his true self to her, somehow... made himself vulnerable, and then love will inevitably follow. The thing is, Lucy, I never felt like that about any of the girls here. Pleasant enough girls, but not the smallest desire to talk to any of them about clouds or the majesty of the ocean."

Lucinda laughed, but when Titus had gone and she was alone with her flower vases, she was thoughtful. She understood what he meant. The exchanges between men and women tended to the superficial, but when acquaintanceship deepens into friendship... when a man exposes his true self... makes himself vulnerable...

Inevitably, her thoughts turned to Captain Edgerton. They had not talked about clouds, but their conversation had been deep, for all that. He had talked about war and mistresses and the nature of men in such an open way, with nothing at all held back. Did that mean he was falling in love with her, as she was with him? Yet he could be so reserved, sometimes, almost avoiding her company. That was not the behaviour of a man on the brink of love.

She could make nothing of it.

~~~~~

SEPTEMBER

Hurtsmere Castle settled back into its usual routine. The three countesses sat in the Lesser Chamber each morning, according to their custom. Lady Morpeth wrote her letters and then snoozed. The Dowager Countess made notes from whatever book she was reading, although what she ever did with her notes, Lucinda could not say. The Young Countess stitched away, making gowns or cloaks or tiny reticules for one or other of the granddaughters. Lord Morpeth disappeared into his study, although his attorney sons called so frequently that it was to be supposed that he had not yet abandoned his interest in the law.

Lucinda was listless. Now that the great celebration was over, there was little for her to organise. The servants were perfectly capable of running the house without any help whatsoever, and no one was minded for even so much as a dinner for neighbours. "Let us recover a little before we start entertaining again, Luce," Lady Morpeth said plaintively. Apart from surreptitiously inviting the retired general from the adjoining estate to drink his tea with them of an evening so that Lord Morpeth might have a piquet partner, there was nothing at all for her to do.

The second morning after the departures, she set out to ride before breakfast. It was a damp, drizzly day, but she did not mind a little rain. She wore her oldest pelisse and hat, which would not suffer too badly if they became wet, and made a full circuit of the perimeter track.

It was dreary riding on her own, she discovered. She was not one for meaningless chit-chat, but one could indulge in a proper conversation on horseback. There was something freeing about the movement and the constant change of vista that inspired more interesting subjects. Or perhaps she was just remembering her meetings with Captain Edgerton. His conversations were always interesting.

That was not a train of thought which could raise her spirits, however. He was gone, and she would not see him again. He had been charming and friendly and treated her as a person worthy of meaningful discussion, but he had never stepped across the line into courtship. It was unutterably sad to consider, but she had never been properly courted. One or two juvenile admirers had never done more than blush and stammer. Walter Swinburn had told her that he could not speak of anything so frivolous as love. And Graham Hesketh had run out of things to say to her in two days. Not only had he never invited her opinion of clouds or the ocean, he had not said anything of interest at all. He had only become loquacious when he was berating her. Thank goodness she had discovered his true character in time!

But she *had* been courted, her heart whispered. Someone, some unknown person, too shy or secretive to declare himself openly, had found a way into her locked room night after night, to leave little gifts on her pillow. He had spoken of admiration and love. What could be clearer? But unless he made himself known, nothing could ever come of it.

The Captain and the Country Cousin

Whoever he was, her secret admirer had gone without revealing himself, and perhaps he never would.

With these depressing thoughts whirring in her head, she returned to the castle and changed for the morning. After breakfast, there was a pleasant discussion with Mrs Philips about the menu for dinner. This was always presented to Lady Morpeth for approval, but since she never made even the smallest change, it was Lucinda's choices which graced the table each evening.

Lucinda wrote her own letters for an hour, by which time the three countesses would be in the Lesser Chamber and she could take in the post. There were a great many heaped up on the silver salver in the entrance hall awaiting her attention. She smiled, for these would be letters of thanks from the last guests to leave, and an excuse for Lady Morpeth to write in return. Not that she needed much excuse.

Sorting the countesses' letters was always an awkward business. All too many correspondents addressed their missives to the Countess of Morpeth when they actually meant the Dowager Countess of Morpeth, or Mary, Countess of Morpeth, and sometimes it would be Mary, Countess of Morpeth when they meant the Dowager, so Lucinda had become adept at recognising handwriting. On this occasion, however, there were too many unfamiliar hands, so the four ladies settled down to the pleasurable business of guessing. The salver was set on a table, and they all gathered around to peer at the letters and try to determine which letter was for which countess.

"This must be from one of the Heskeths," the Young Countess said. "It is franked by Lord Wallasey, you see."

The Captain and the Country Cousin

"It is Everard's hand," Lucinda said. "Oh, here is one from Rowena, Aunt Mary. But this— Oh!"

"What is it, dear?" Lady Morpeth said, looking up in surprise. "You have gone very pale, Lucy. What is the matter?"

"Nothing... nothing..." Why was the room so warm? She could hardly breathe. She dropped the letter in haste, and quickly picked up another. "From Lavinia."

"Ah, she said she would write soon to tell me if the little one is better. Oh, whose hand is this, Lucy? What an interesting style."

"I... I do not..." *Breathe, Lucinda, breathe!* She could not even say she did not recognise it, for were there not two charades and a poem in the same hand resting in a drawer in her bedroom?

"Oh, what a charming letter! It is from Captain Edgerton, and so well written. Oh, but this one is from Lady..."

Lucinda heard nothing more. Her aunt's voice was very far away, barely audible. The three of them were still chattering away, opening letters, reading well-expressed passages, exclaiming over this one or that, but Lucinda could attend to none of it.

Captain Edgerton!

Her mysterious admirer was Captain Edgerton, and in that instant the man of her heart and the romantic giver of gifts collided in spectacular fashion. *There* was a man she could love with a passion, a man who embodied all the physical masculine attributes to attract a lady, who also had the romantic soul she so craved. A man who could dance well and dismount so elegantly from a horse, who could wield a sword like the heroes of old, who could speak with equal facility of swords or mistresses or the habits of his sex, a man who could enter a locked room simply to leave her a single red rose and a few lines of a love poem. A man to whom she could surrender her heart without a single qualm, and be happy forever.

She could not breathe. Her life had changed irrevocably in that instant, and she could not even speak of it. *She could not breathe!*

~~~~~

And so Lucinda waited. Because if Captain Edgerton had sent her all those gifts, then he must — he *must* — care for her in some way, and sooner or later he would write or send a message or come himself, and then she would be happy. She could not be happy without him, she knew that now, and every day, every hour made her more sure of it.

But he did not come. He sent no word, and he did not come, and each night she cried a little more and woke in greater despair.

The days passed and the wretched, tear-filled nights, and nothing brought her any relief. Aunt Mary asked her if she were well, and she answered that of course she was, for nothing ever ailed her, and why should she not be well? And Aunt Mary smiled worriedly and said no more. Yet every night Lucinda cried hot tears for him into the pillow where he had left the tokens of his love.

The Captain and the Country Cousin

One day Uncle Quentin called her to his study and sat her beside the fire. "I have had a letter from Walter Swinburn," he said. "He wishes you to know that he regrets the way you parted last month, and asks if there is any way I might prevail upon you to accept his suit. He enclosed a letter for you, my dear."

"What does it say?"

"I have not read it. Do you wish to have it? I was under the impression that your parting was final."

"So was I," she said. "Do you think I should read it?"

He smiled a little ruefully, steepling his fingers. "My dear Lucy, I know your opinion of him, and I cannot think that a letter now, no matter how eloquently worded, will change it. However, it would be a courtesy to read what he has to say."

"Very well, then."

Unfolding the letter, she read, 'My dear Miss Willerton-Forbes, I write to beg your forgiveness for my unfortunate words at our last encounter, which I deeply regret. Believe me when I tell you that I would unsay them if I could. I spoke without considering the effect of such hasty expressions, and upon long thought I must conclude that I have gravely misled you if you now believe that I have no regard for you. Nothing could be further from the truth. As the object of all my hopes for matrimonial happiness, it would be extraordinary if I did not hold you in the greatest esteem and respect, and I would willingly place you in the position of utmost reverence as the chosen helpmeet of my life and the mother of my children. I beg that you will grant me a further interview to convince you *of my steadfast devotion, which only death may curtail. Yours in hope, Walter Swinburn.'*

"No, it does not change my opinion," she said sadly. "He still cannot tell me he loves me."

The earl smiled. "Would you marry Walter if he spoke passionately to you?"

"No," she said decisively. "I would not marry Walter if his love burned as bright as a thousand suns. He is a good man and a worthy one, but I will never marry him, and a sensible man would have accepted that years ago. I suspect his attachment arises more from a lack of imagination. He settled on me as the most suitable candidate and he *still* thinks me suitable. It is beyond his comprehension that I might find him too dull for words."

"Is that the problem?" the earl said. "I concede, he is excessively dull. But what then are you looking for in a husband?"

"I want a man who excites me, Uncle, with whom I would never be bored. A romantic man, with poetry in his soul. A man who adores me, and tells me so."

"Hmm. Not all men are... articulate in that way. A man may feel very deeply, yet be unable to say the words."

"Then he must show it, if he cannot speak."

"Even that can be difficult. For an arrogant man like Graham Hesketh, it does not occur to him that you would turn him down. Walter Swinburn is arrogant, too, in his way. To both of them, the offer is a good one, you should be grateful to receive it and happy to accept. But a man who is truly in love, who sees his darling as a person to be valued for herself and not merely for her dowry or her beauty — well, he will not be arrogant at all. He will feel deeply unworthy to marry his love, and will not imagine that she may be waiting and hoping for him to speak. Such a man needs some encouragement to speak openly."

Lucinda had never heard her uncle speak this way before, and by the conscious expression on his face, she knew he spoke from experience. "You?" she said softly.

"Oh yes. I was desperately in love with my Mary, but I dared not speak, for what could she possibly see in a man like me? She was so lovely, so gentle and kind, she could marry as high as she pleased, and why would she even look at a humble attorney?" He chuckled. "One day she took me aside after church and said to me, *'Well, Quentin? Are you going to get on with it, because I should quite like to be married by Michaelmas.'* And so we were."

Lucinda laughed, but she took the point. A man might need some encouragement to speak... for the first time in a long time, she felt a glimmer of hope. But how could it be done? *Breathe, Lucinda.*

"Shall I write to Swinburn on your behalf?" the earl said. "He must accept a final dismissal from me, I believe, and there is no reason for you to be troubled any further with the fellow."

"Thank you, that would be a kindness."

"Good. So that is settled. Have you heard from Pettigrew? He is planning a celebration for his birthday, quite a big affair by all accounts. All his friends will be there. Your aunt and I are minded to go. Do you want to come with us? I know you hate London, but just this once would not hurt, and you could do a little shopping with your aunt. She would be glad of your company."

Breathe... "Why not?"

~~~~~

London was just as it always was, loud, dirty and dismal, not improved by a constant light drizzle. For once, Lucinda did not care. She had only one object in view and the horrors of town could not deter her. She was determined to risk all on one desperate throw of the dice, and confront Captain Edgerton. And then she would see what came of it. If nothing, then she was no worse off than before, after all, and she was miserable enough not to care about the humiliation.

Pettigrew's house was tucked away discreetly just off Curzon Street. He shared it with Sir Rathbone and Lady Willerton-Forbes, and whichever members of the family happened to be visiting town. Strangely, Lucinda and the earl and countess were the only visitors this time, despite the planned celebrations. And when had Pettigrew ever noticed his birthday before? It was not even a special one.

Lucinda had been too agitated when packing to do more than throw a few gowns into her box. Now she found that she had brought nothing she liked, and ended by picking one at random. What did it matter anyway? She was not there to entice the captain with her charms, for if he were susceptible he would have fallen at her feet at the castle. As she went down to the drawing room, she consoled herself with the thought that she could yet back away from this venture. But still she shivered and pulled her silk shawl tighter about her.

She positioned herself on the far side of the room, with a good view of the arriving guests, but not so close that her quarry would be forced to speak to her at once. Her quarry! How cold and scheming that sounded. But so it was, in a way. She wanted him to come to her, if he would, and if he would not, or took his time over it, then she would know what to think. But if he came at once... *please let him come at once.*

He was one of the earliest to arrive, bringing a small gift for Pettigrew, which made him laugh, and then greeting Lord and Lady Morpeth. Then he turned and looked around the room... he saw her... his face changed... She could not read his expression, but he locked his eyes on hers and made his way steadily across the room, ignoring at least two people who addressed him, until he stood before her.

"Miss Willerton-Forbes, what a pleasure to see you again! I had no expectation of it, knowing your aversion to town, but I am delighted that your affection for your cousin allowed you to overcome it."

She was so unsettled herself that she could not be sure, but she thought his voice was a little unsteady, and his usual smile was absent. Was that a good sign or a bad one? She could not tell and at that moment did not much care. She was about to jump off the cliff, and his feelings were less meaningful to her than her own turbulent mixture of terror, determination and hope. She must not give up hope.

"I did not come here for Pettigrew," she said breathlessly.

The Captain and the Country Cousin

Surprise on his face. "Oh... then... may I ask...?"

"I came because of you, Captain. I should like to talk to you, if I may. Would you attend me here at... say, nine o'clock tomorrow morning?"

"Oh... yes... It would be my pleasure."

And still she could not read his expression. She could not guess whether it would be a pleasure to either of them.

9: A Summons

He was punctual to the minute, as she had expected. She received him in the morning room, the ladies' sanctuary, where the gentlemen of the house would not venture, and the other ladies not before noon. He greeted her with apparent sangfroid, as always, and she had no idea what to make of that.

"Good morning, Captain Edgerton. Thank you for coming."

He bowed over her hand in typically flamboyant style. "It is my pleasure, Miss Willerton-Forbes. How may I serve you?"

There was no point beating about the bush. "I should like to know, sir, why you left roses and poems and all sorts of other nonsense on my pillow during your recent stay at Hurtsmere Castle."

His eyebrows rose at this assault, but he answered readily, as if he had been expecting the question. "Why, to bring a smile to your face, no more than that. A little pleasure at the end of a long day."

"You do not deny it, then?"

The Captain and the Country Cousin

"I will not insult you by dissembling, madam. Those little gifts were indeed my doing."

"But how?" she burst out. "My door was locked."

"Was it? But your window was not."

"You came in through the window?"

"You have a balcony. My room was two across from yours, also with a balcony, and the ivy is strong."

She gave a little gasp at his insouciance. *The ivy is strong!* To speak so casually of clambering about three floors above the ground. "But you could have been killed! You risked your life to put flowers and poems on my pillow."

"No, no! The risk was negligible, and it seemed worth it to give you a little happiness. You worked so hard for the benefit of your relations, who seemed to take your efforts for granted. It seemed to me that they did not value you as you deserved. I wished you to know that there was one person in that house, at least, who saw what you did and appreciated it. I meant no harm by my actions, and am grieved indeed to have distressed you in any way. That was very far from my intent."

"No harm, sir?" For an instant she could scarcely breathe — how dared he speak so? She spun away from him and walked across the room, only to turn back at once. She would not be fobbed off! "No harm? To leave tokens of affection, poetry and flowers and hearts, to speak of admiration and... and *love* — and then to depart without a word? To give no indication of any further attentions? To leave me, sir, in a suspense of confusion and wondering about the matter of who, and how, and mostly why? How could you do such a thing? It was unkind in you, very unkind."

She spoke with more heat than she had intended, but it had an immediate effect upon him. The insouciance in his face was gone, replaced by concern. He crossed the room in two strides, and lifted her hand in his.

"You are right, entirely right. I allowed my enthusiasm for the adventure to carry me beyond what was proper, it is true. I should have been... more restrained, perhaps, but I could not tell... You seemed so composed, so unaffected that I assumed you took my offerings in the same light-hearted way I made them. I had no idea that my feeble efforts to raise your spirits would cause such turmoil in your mind and disturb your equanimity. I do most sincerely beg your forgiveness for my ineptness. How may I make it right? What would you have me do? If there is any way in which I might make amends, I would have you tell me of it at once."

"And you would do it — whatever I ask?" she said, startled. The warmth of his hand on hers was causing her head to spin.

"If it be within my power."

Did she dare? But was this not why she had come? It was too opportune an opening to be refused. "There is but one way in which a gentleman may make amends to a lady for raising expectations."

There was a brief flash of emotion on his face — surprise? or was it delight? — before he schooled his countenance. "Marriage? Then let it be so."

The Captain and the Country Cousin

She gave a little gasp at his instant surrender, then laughed. "You have excellent manners, Captain."

He smiled too, his eyes twinkling in the way she had come to love. "So I have always been told. If you expected me to object or find excuses, then I am very sorry to disappoint you. Did you intend to punish me? If so, I must tell you that marriage to you would hardly be a penance. You are as beautiful, as elegant, as charming a woman as I have ever met. I should be delighted to meet you at the altar rail."

"This is the strangest conversation!" she burst out, fully alive to the forwardness of her own behaviour, yet reluctant in the extreme to let him go. She had not truly intended to trap him into marriage, merely to provoke a declaration, yet now she felt both joy and guilt for her actions, in equal measure. "I cannot think you mean what you say, and I have no wish to take an unwilling husband."

"Have I not made it clear that I am not unwilling?" he said. "Oh, do you wish me to do it properly?" He dropped gracefully to one knee, her hand still in his. "Miss Willerton-Forbes, would you do me the inestimable honour of becoming my wife?"

Excellent manners indeed, and so smoothly spoken. He was never at a loss, yet he was a puzzle, too. Could he truly be so complaisant in a matter which upended his entire life? Did he then care for her, in some way, or was he gracefully accepting the inevitable? This was not a moment for misunderstandings. Whether he held her in some affection that could be built upon, with time, or whether he was indifferent but willing to pretend otherwise, she must know his heart, once and for all.

The Captain and the Country Cousin

Withdrawing her hand, she moved to a sofa and sat. "I cannot make you out, Captain. You speak sweet words, but I know not whether you mean them."

"You want to know the truth?" he said, rising, and sitting at the other end of the sofa. "Then I will tell you this, with no pretence. It would be the greatest pleasure and privilege to call you my wife, and there is not an ounce of reluctance in me. Not an iota. It would delight me beyond measure to devote the rest of my life to making you happy, and I flatter myself I could do it, too. You would not find me a troublesome husband, I assure you. So long as I have enough activity to keep me busy and you to come home to each night, I should be perfectly content. But beyond that you must not press me. Do not speak to me of love, or ask me to do so."

That was honesty indeed, and she could scarce complain at such openness, having explicitly invited it. Breathlessly, she said, "Very well. It shall be as you wish." He would be hers! She wanted to shout with joy, but dared not. He wanted no sign of affection from her. She lowered her eyes.

He slid nearer, and took her hand again. "Are you disappointed in me? You must not be. You said that I speak sweet words but you cannot tell whether I mean them. Luce, I *always* mean what I say. Oh, I may exaggerate occasionally, or embellish my little stories, the better to entertain the company, but when I pay a lady a compliment, I always speak the truth. When I say I am perfectly willing to marry you, that you are the most beautiful creature I ever saw, that I would be proud to be your husband, I am being entirely honest. But if you want me to whisper words of love in your ear, I cannot do it." A hesitation, then he went on, "If we are to be married, we must be open with each other, so may I tell you why?"

Mutely she nodded.

"My father and mother were the most devoted couple in the world," he began. "They adored each other, and showed their adoration to the world. They spent almost every hour of every day together, and were miserable if ever they had to be apart. They cared for my brother and me, too, but in an absent-minded, distracted sort of way. They had little time for anyone but each other. Then my mother died, and it was almost as quick as that. One day she felt a little unwell, the second day there was raging fever and the third day she died. My father... well, he died, too, in a way. He lives still, but a shell of his former self. He sits by the fire all day, staring at the chair where my mother always sat, as if he waits for her to return to him. My brother and his wife take care of him but it is a ghastly business. I swore that *my* heart would never be so vulnerable, that I would wrap it up so tightly that no one should ever know what I truly feel, or whether I feel anything at all. That way I would be protected, and be able to get through this treacherous world with my sanity intact. Do you understand?"

"I think so, yes." But she was not sure that she did. Was he saying that he felt nothing for her? Or was there some affection there, but he dared not show it? It was confusing.

"Can you live with that? Can you accept me as I am, and not expect more than I am able to give you?"

She nodded, full of some emotion she could not quite name. Elation, because he would be hers, but was that also a twinge of disappointment? She was only just now realising how much she had hoped that he would fall at her feet with a declaration of undying love. This prosaic negotiation, for all his carefully worded compliments, was not what she had expected.

"Then shall we call ourselves betrothed?" he said, smiling in that heart-stopping way.

She nodded again, then was struck by a sudden thought. "You wanted to marry a great fortune and a title. So Pettigrew said."

He laughed. "You are an Honourable, so that will do very well for boasting purposes. I shall just have to maintain a discreet silence on the subject of great fortunes."

"I cannot claim to have a *great* fortune, but I am not penniless," she said. "I have fifteen thousand and a small estate, and Aunt Guinevere has promised me something, too."

"But that is excellent!" he cried. "Now I shall be able to tell everyone that I married both fortune and title, and hint at the expectation, too. Perfect!"

She laughed too, but he was so frustrating! As slippery as an eel, sometimes. He would not be pinned down, and at that moment it was too much to be borne. Impulsively she moved along the sofa, pulled him towards her and drew him into a kiss.

Oh, the delight of his lips! So soft, so tender, so gentle. Warmth swelled inside her, seeping from somewhere deep in her chest and spreading slowly and inexorably to every part of her body. He was hers! Finally, after so many anxious days and weepy nights he was holding her in his arms, one arm wrapped tight around her waist, his free hand tangled in her hair, stroking, caressing. Finally, finally, she could release the torrent of emotion that had been bottled up inside her. He might not wish her to speak of love, perhaps, but she could *show* him, she could express her feelings just as well — better! — in one glorious kiss that went on and on...

She never wanted it to end, but eventually, breathlessly, they moved apart and she gazed into his dear face — his fascinating lips, his smooth forehead, his eyes... Oh, his eyes! She was looking straight into his heart, and what she saw there made her catch her breath. Such a light in his eyes as she could not mistake. He could not speak of love, but it was there all the same. And at that moment all the confusions and darkness of the last few weeks dropped away, as if she had successfully negotiated the turbulent rapids and arrived at a pool of deep contentment.

He exhaled a ragged breath. "Good God, Luce, you must marry me *at once*, do you hear? A licence... we must get a licence... or shall we elope?"

A gurgle of laughter escaped her. Now *his* passion was sweeping over him, and she was the rational one. "What nonsense you do talk, Michael. I must have time to get my wedding clothes, and get the settlement drawn up. You are marrying into a family of lawyers, you know, and a marriage settlement is a serious business to them, not a matter to be rushed."

He let out his breath slowly, as if begrudging the return to prosaic matters. "I suppose you are right. What time will

Lord Morpeth be up? I shall need to talk to him as soon as may be."

"He will be dressed already. I shall send word to him."

Lucinda waited in the hall while her uncle interviewed her future husband in the book room. He had not the power to forbid it, but he might still dislike the match. He was not so stuffy as to look down on a man who was a former soldier and now a horse trader, but he might suspect his motives. Did Michael have any money beyond his wages from Tattersall's? An army pension, presumably, but not much else. She had never thought to ask.

A quarter of an hour passed by, and then another before Michael emerged, with Uncle Quentin at his side. They were both smiling, thank goodness!

"Lucy, step inside a moment, if you please. Shut the door. Now then, this is a surprise, eh? Well, Mary suspected something was afoot, and set about getting you to London to settle matters, but I was afraid you might be out of luck. He did not seem to me... but I was wrong, I am happy to say. But tell me, child — you have had suitors enough, so why this one in particular?"

How difficult it was to answer such a question. "I cannot say in rational terms," she said slowly. "I cannot point to one thing or another... or one moment or another... and say, there, that is what did it. But a point was reached where I knew that I could not be happy without him."

"You love him?"

An easier one. "Yes."

The Captain and the Country Cousin

"And does he love you?"

She thought of the rose and the heart-shaped stone and the poem, and smiled. She recalled his kiss, and blushed. "Yes, he does."

"Then I am satisfied. He would not answer me directly on that point, saying only that it was a private matter between the two of you, but I could not approve of a match where there was affection on only one side. However, he is perfectly eligible in every other way. He has fifteen hundred a year and—"

"Does he?"

The earl chuckled. "He made a considerable fortune in India, seemingly, although he does not bruit it about. He is unassuming in that way, and I like that about him. He is the elder son, although the family home will go to his younger brother, who now lives in it, but since you have Rudgewood House, that need not concern you. I congratulate you, niece. It will please me greatly to see you settled at last. You will not want to wait long, I imagine. Should you like me to draw up the settlements for you? I am not yet so out of the habit of such work."

"No, indeed, Uncle, it is not fitting. Pettigrew will do it. He loves such work, and he rarely has the opportunity nowadays, so grand as he is getting."

The earl laughed. "True enough, but he is Edgerton's friend, so I will get one of his brothers to look over it, just to be safe. Well, this calls for a celebration. Fetch your young man in again, Lucy, and let us all drink a toast to your future felicity."

The Captain and the Country Cousin

~~~~~

Michael returned to Hurtsmere Castle only the day before the wedding. Lucinda had so longed for this moment, had imagined it so many times, had even dreamt of it, that when it came it was inevitably a disappointment. He smiled, he bowed over her hand, he even raised it to his lips, but there was nothing more. She had not expected words of love, but she had hoped to see again that fire in his eyes, the light of undeniable love shining upon her. It was not there.

Then she began to doubt herself. She had been so certain of him, so sure that he loved her. Was she mistaken in that? All through the afternoon, when they sat snugly in the Lesser Chamber with the countesses, and then through dinner with the family and local worthies, she pondered the point. All the time he was affable, he exerted all his powers to amuse and entertain her, and yet there was nothing in the least lover-like in any of it.

When the ladies withdrew after dinner, she had time to compose her thoughts somewhat. Deliberately, she recalled their conversation in London, when she had berated him for his romantic gifts and he had, without the slightest protest, agreed to marry her. No, he had *offered* to marry her, and gone out of his way to assure her that he was entirely willing. What had he said? *'It would be the greatest pleasure and privilege to call you my wife.'* And then he had kissed her... She closed her eyes for a moment, remembering, allowing the warmth to spread through her again. That kiss was all the proof she needed that he loved her.

The Captain and the Country Cousin

"Lucy? Are you all right, dear?" the Young Countess said.

Laughing, Lucinda said, "Perfectly all right, Lady Morpeth."

"You look a little flushed. I hope you are not feverish."

"Of course she is feverish! It is the eve before her wedding," the Dowager Countess said, and the ladies all laughed indulgently.

The gentlemen came in soon after, and Michael sought her straight away, a smile on his lips. Oh, his lips... how they tantalised her! She could not wait to feel them again, to feel his passion, just as strong as hers. Tomorrow... then he would be hers at last, his love would be hers.

Later that night, he escorted her back to her tower, but to her surprise, he led her first to the Long Gallery. Holding the candelabrum high, he walked down the full length of it, the flickering flames setting the many blades afire on the walls.

"This is my favourite room in the castle," he said, his voice soft and low.

"Because of the swords?"

"That and... memories." Setting the candelabrum down on a table, he stepped close to her, his hands cupping her face. "Tomorrow everything will change. No second thoughts?"

"None. You?"

"No." A hesitation. "Luce..." he began, and then sighed. "I wish I could say everything that I feel inside. You deserve that, but I… I cannot do it. I just cannot. I have hidden myself away behind a wall of flirting and joking and story-telling and relentless activity, and I have been wrapped up tight for so many years that I do not know if I can ever unwrap myself again."

"Sshh." Gently she placed one finger on his lips. "I understand. You asked me to accept you as you are, and I do. You asked me not to expect more from you than you were able to give, and I do not. I see what is in your heart, and that is enough. I do not need you to say it, I can see it in your eyes, and in the things you do. Love is not in words, Michael, it is in deeds. Leave me a rose on my pillow every now and then, and I shall know what that means."

He exhaled slowly. "Then we need never speak of this again."

"Let it be our little secret," she whispered.

He nodded, and there it was again, that joyous light in his eyes that was just for her alone. She need never doubt his love, not for a moment. She would never doubt it again.

He escorted her to the foot of the north-eastern tower, kissed her formally on both cheeks as the footman discreetly averted his eyes, and hoped she would sleep well. Then he strode away without a backwards glance.

Betty was unusually garrulous that night, so it was some time before Lucinda could escape the dressing room, ready for bed. Was there a slight chill in the air of the bedroom, or was it her imagination? Smiling, she carried her candle to the bed.

The Captain and the Country Cousin

There on the pillow lay a single red rose.

Burying her nose in the soft petals to catch the elusive fragrance, she murmured to herself, "I love you too, Michael Edgerton."

Impulsively, she went to the window, pulled open the door and stepped out onto the tiny balcony. He was there, on the next balcony but one, the gleam of his smile clearly visible in the darkness. Raising his fingers to his lips, he blew her a kiss, and she reciprocated. Then, with a wave, he was gone.

Laughter bubbled up inside her. Michael had his odd quirks, but he was gallant and honourable and deliciously romantic, in his own way, and life with him would never, ever be dull. She was the luckiest girl alive.

Epilogue

Lavinia sighed with sentimental fervour. "Oh, Lucy, that is *so* romantic! Roses! And poems... gifts... something every night. And to climb across on the ivy! Heavens, no wonder you fell in love with him."

"That and the sword fighting," Lucinda said, laughing. "You have no idea how distractingly attractive Michael is when he has a sword in his hand. I know people look at him and see a funny little man, with his flamboyant ways and his outrageous stories, but I see a warrior with the soul of a poet."

"Does he still put roses on your pillow?"

"Oh yes," Lucinda said softly. "Flowers and poems and sweet things and all sorts of silly little gifts. When he is away, he writes to me every day, when he can, and sometimes twice a day. Even when we are apart, I know that he is thinking of me, and that he loves me."

"But does he ever tell you so?"

Lucinda blushed. "Well... sometimes. There are moments when his defensive walls crumble and he can say all that is in his heart."

"How lucky we are to have husbands who love us well," Lavinia said. "But both of them needed a jolt to actually propose."

"Wilbraham too?" Lucinda said. "How did you persuade him to get on with it?"

She laughed merrily. "I got Papa to talk to him. To be honest, I was far too embarrassed to say anything to him myself, but he had been hanging around for positively weeks, looking at me with those wistful eyes of his, like a puppy. I knew what *I* wanted, and I was tolerably sure what he wanted, and Papa had already made enquiries as to money and so forth, so what was he waiting for? So Papa arranged a day's shooting and brought it up casually while they were out, man to man. And Will came back to the house with him and proposed on the spot. Some men are so diffident, they need a bit of a nudge... or a good shove, in Will's case. But Michael is not at all diffident, I would have said. He is not arrogant in the least, but he understands his own worth very well. So why did he leave all those romantic love tokens on your pillow, and yet not say a word to you directly, when he clearly adored you from the start?"

Lucinda laughed. "Naturally, I asked him that, but it was a long time before he would tell me. Can you believe it, he was afraid that I would laugh at him if he proposed?"

"Laugh at him? But why would you do that? He must have known that you— Oh, but you are always so serene, so outwardly composed, that I daresay he did not realise you felt the same way. But still, even if you had not, you would never have *laughed* at him!"

"No, for that would be terribly rag-mannered of me. But you see, Michael is so very conscious of his height. He knows perfectly well that he is never taken seriously, so short as he is, which is why he responds by doing everything with a bit of a swagger. He plays up to it rather. But there he was, falling in love with a woman whom he felt was above him on the social scale and also literally above him in height, and he was terrified that he would appear ridiculous to me. He did not mind being rejected, or at least not much, but he could not bear it if I laughed, or worse still, pitied him. I had given him no open encouragement, so he decided it was quite hopeless, foolish man, and went back to London without saying a word. I only found out by sheer chance that he was my secret admirer."

"Hardly by chance," Lavinia said. "Michael knew perfectly well when he wrote his letter to Lady Morpeth that you would see it and recognise the hand, and then you would know."

Lucinda opened her mouth to object and immediately closed it again with a snap. "Huh! The sneaky fellow! No wonder he was so at ease when I came hurtling up to town after him, for he had been expecting it... or hoping, perhaps. He left me all his romantic offerings, then departed, knowing that I would discover his identity almost at once. And then he waited to see what I would do. And in fact he gave *me* a nudge... or a shove, perhaps. He persuaded Pettigrew to hold a birthday celebration, something he has never done before or since, to give me a reason to go to town. Pettigrew wrote to Aunt Mary, to make sure I went. Oh, it was all arranged!"

"I daresay he wanted to be quite sure of your affection before he declared himself," Lavinia said, laughing too. "That is very sensible, to my mind. A man likes to know that his addresses will be welcome."

"Except that he had me so agitated that *I* was the one who made the declaration," Lucinda cried. "All he had to do was to accept gracefully, which I acknowledge he did beautifully. His manners are impeccable. Oh dear! I feel very… managed, I suppose." She laughed. "He is very clever, that husband of mine."

The footman came in just then with the day's letters.

"There you are, Lucy, two for you from Michael," Lavinia said.

Eagerly, Lucinda tore them open. The first was just the usual chatter from the village where he was staying, but the second was a surprise. "He wants me to go there," she said, astonished. "They are to stay for some time, so they have taken a house and Michael wishes me to join them."

"How lovely," Lavinia said. "He must be missing you very badly."

"Possibly, but his primary concern is his stomach. I am to take Mrs Cromer and Lisa the pastry cook, and he has sent me a list of the supplies he wants from the cellar. I am to keep house for him and his friends while they conduct their investigations."

The Captain and the Country Cousin

"Shall you like being away from your own home?" Lavinia said cautiously.

"Oh yes! It is a very small village, so it will not be overwhelming, and I shall be with Michael, which will make me very happy. He sounds very anxious for me to go. He writes, *'Do say you will come,'* three times, at least."

"Ah, he is very fond of you, Lucy."

Lucinda laughed. "Fond? Too tame a word altogether. He *adores* me, and I him, and in a few days we shall be together again, and the world will be in perfect alignment. I cannot wait!" She shivered in satisfaction.

THE END

Thanks for reading!

If you have enjoyed reading this book, please consider writing a short review on Amazon. You can find out the latest news and sign up for the mailing list at my website at http://marykingswood.co.uk

Family tree: Hi-res version available at my website at http://marykingswood.co.uk

A note on historical accuracy: I have endeavoured to stay true to the spirit of Regency times, and have avoided taking too many liberties or imposing modern sensibilities on my characters. The book is not one of historical record, but I've tried to make it reasonably accurate. However, I'm not perfect! If you spot a historical error, I'd very much appreciate knowing about it so that I can correct it and learn from it. Thank you!

About Captain Edgerton and Mr Willerton-Forbes: Captain Edgerton, formerly of the East India Company Army and later of Tattersall's, and lawyer Mr Willerton-Forbes first met in *Lord Augustus,* book 3 of the *Sons of the Marquess* series, when they were helping the Duke of Dunmorton with his late son's affairs. The two became friends, and found themselves working together on a number of murders and other crimes and mysterious events throughout the *Sisters of Woodside, Silver Linings* and *Strangers* series.

Dates and times: For those who like to know, the main part of this story takes place after the end of the *Sons of the Marquess* series, and before the first book of the *Sisters of Woodside* series. The Prologue and Epilogue take place during the *Strangers* series, between books 2 and 3. It can be read on its own, however.

About my books: Here's a complete list of my series to date and proposed:

The Daughters of Allamont Hall (6 books + a novella)

Sons of the Marquess (5 books + a novella)

Sisters of Woodside Mysteries (5 books + a novella)

Silver Linings Mysteries (6 books + a novella)

Strangers (6 books + a novella)

The Mercer's House (6 books + 2 novellas)

Any questions about the series? You can email me at mary@marykingswood.co.uk. I'd love to hear from you!

About the author

I write traditional Regency romances under the pen name Mary Kingswood, and epic fantasy as Pauline M Ross. I live in the beautiful Highlands of Scotland with my husband. I like chocolate, whisky, my Kindle, massed pipe bands, long leisurely lunches, chocolate, going places in my campervan, eating pizza in Italy, summer nights that never get dark, wood fires in winter, chocolate, the view from the study window looking out over the Moray Firth and the Black Isle to the mountains beyond. And chocolate. I dislike driving on motorways, cooking, shopping, hospitals.

Acknowledgements

Thanks go to:

My readers: who asked to learn more about Captain Edgerton. This story is for you!

Shayne Rutherford of Darkmoon Graphics for the cover design.

My beta reader: Barbara Daniels Dena

Last, but definitely not least, my first reader: Amy Ross.

Made in the USA
Monee, IL
20 July 2022